DEATH STOPS THE FROLIC

GEORGE BELLAIRS

AGORA BOOKS

ABOUT THE AUTHOR

George Bellairs was the pseudonym of Harold Blundell (1902—1982). He was, by day, a Manchester bank manager with close connections to the University of Manchester. He is often referred to as the English Simenon, as his detective stories combine wicked crimes and classic police procedurals set in quaint villages.

He was born in Lancashire and married Gladys Mabel Roberts in 1930. He was a devoted Francophile and travelled there frequently, writing for English newspapers and magazines and weaving French towns into his fiction.

Bellairs' first mystery, *Littlejohn on Leave* (1941), introduced his series detective, Detective Inspector Thomas Littlejohn. Full of scandal and intrigue, the series peeks inside small towns in the mid twentieth century, and Littlejohn is injected with humour, intelligence and compassion.

He died on the Isle of Man in April 1982 just before his eightieth birthday.

ALSO BY GEORGE BELLAIRS

Devious Murder

Fear Round About

Close All Roads to Sospel

The Downhill Ride of Leeman Popple

An Old Man Dies

Death Stops the Frolic

GEORGE BELLAIRS

This edition published in 2020 by Agora Books

First published in 1943 as *Turmoil in Zion* in Great Britain by John Gifford Limited

Agora Books is a division of Peters Fraser + Dunlop Ltd

55 New Oxford Street, London WC1A 1BS

TO DAD

1

THE TURMOIL BEGINS

To the west of the Great North Road and just where it chops off a portion of the eastern fringe of Brentshire, there lies a district of England which has given its name to a fine breed of sheep, a heavy-cropping tomato, an inferior mangel-wurzel and a now obsolete form of the ague found there before the marshes were drained. In a spot so prolific in bucolic products, labels, and all the splendours attaching to them, one would hardly expect to find a manufacturing town. Yet, the tourist who blindly follows the by-road from Sticksey to Langley St Nicholas, ignorant of the fact that between those two idyllic retreats lies a short but concentrated area of smoke, noise, and feverish activity, is in for a surprise. Before he knows where he is, he is sucked into the commercial whirlpool of Swarebridge. If he timed his arrival by night, he was, until the outbreak of war, greeted in neon by "Pogsley's Snugsleep Blankets," blazing in red and blue from each chimney of the three great factories there. For, Pogsley is Swarebridge, and Swarebridge is Pogsley.

It will be as well for us to get over the origins and topography of Swarebridge before the reader wearies. It is obvious that the place lies on the River Sware and that there is a bridge!

Twenty years ago, the car of Mr Samuel Pogsley broke down on that bridge, which at the time carried the main road to the village, small and neat, of about 600 people. It happened that Mr Pogsley was seeking a site for his new blanket mills, so whilst his chauffeur changed a wheel, his master viewed the landscape o'er, took a sample bottle of water from the Sware, went on his way and a week later made up his mind to enter the promised land.

The village gradually spread as blankets brought it fame, prosperity and the itch for constant chopping and changing which follows progress. Two thousand new operatives arrived by degrees as the new mills were, one by one, put into commission. Houses, packed together and flung-up irrespective of quality or appearance, swarmed in every direction, and all the usual urban services of transport, sewers, lighting, entertainment and sale of stimulants rapidly followed. In four years, the populations had grown to 10,000 and every market day another two or three thousand countryfolk rushed in from miles around to gape, buy, sell and take their pleasures.

The three new mills were built on the banks of the Sware, houses sprang up all round them, overflowed on to the main road, hitherto the village street and now the main shopping centre, and the railway crowned the venture by bringing a branch line, which as Mr Pogsley, who opened it, declared would link Swarebridge with civilisation. He forgot to mention that it would also reduce the freight on supplying civilisation with Snugsleep Blankets.

When Swarebridge became a borough, Mr Pogsley was the charter mayor. On the following Sunday, Zion Chapel was formally opened and dedicated to the propagation of the Gospel on the lines laid down by the denomination of which Pogsley was a luminary. With the exception of the established church, to which the original natives of Swarebridge were almost fanatically attached (especially after the advent of Pogsley!) and barring twenty-two Methodists, who held their meetings in a corrugated-iron hut, the operatives of the new mills mainly attended Zion. The reason for this unanimity was that in his choice of employees for blanket-making, Mr Pogsley favoured those of his own spiritual leanings. Some of other faiths, of course, saw the light and were converted to become pillars of Zion after a preliminary interview for a job. That, then, accounted for the presence of the great chapel in the High Street, which led the religious life of Swarebridge.

The edifice itself was planned by the great Pogsley but was conceived at the worst time of ecclesiastical architecture, when so-called modern styles closely resembling picture-palaces were emerging from the womb of ugly Victorian monstrosities and parturition was not complete. Zion combined the worst of both worlds.

His work on earth ended and the chapel properly endowed, Mr Samuel Pogsley passed-on, leaving a will in which he expressed a wish to be buried beneath the pulpit in Zion. This ambition was immediately squashed by the local sanitary inspector, a young newcomer who knew not Pogsley. So, the founder of Swarebridge's prosperity and the architect of its spiritual life for years to come, was buried in a large mausoleum at the back of the church, which necessitated the re-planning of that area to the tune of transplanting the outdoor lavatories and creating a grove of rhododendrons round the new home of the great one. Thus, in death, Zion and Pogsley were not divided.

Let us now return to the present.

In the month of October 1941, at two o'clock in the afternoon, the congregation of Zion gathered to celebrate the twenty-fifth anniversary of the foundation of their bethel. This consisted of a procession of the members and adherents, young and old, with a brass band at the front and an ancient Victoria containing four superannuated members of the church who were unable to make the tour on foot, bringing up the rear. The concourse marched round the town, halting now and then to sing lustily and to flaunt its numbers before the established churchmen and the forty-two Methodists, ten of whose original twenty-two had died or seceded to Pogsley, but who had been replaced threefold by converts. Having sung vociferously at four places, including the parish church and the Methodist tin tabernacle, the Zionists returned with good appetites to their schoolroom, where five hundred sat down to a meal consisting of ham, tongue, brown and white bread, jam-cake, celery and tea.

A celebrated preacher, Rev Archibald Cowslip, MA, PhD, Principal of Arrowford College, was preaching the anniversary sermons on the morrow, but at the tea party the resident minister, Rev B Augustus Partington, officiated. He was tall, pale and suffered in secret from an inferiority complex, for he was a failed BA, BD, of London. He compensated for this, however, by an aggressive spirit and a shrill, masterful delivery. He rose, called for grace and, without waiting for the piano, for he was eager to be getting at the ham, began to sing to the tune *Pogsley*. The rest joined in:

> *"Lord, be present at our feasting,*
> *Here abide, Thy children bless.*
> *Grant us water in life's desert,*
> *Manna in its wilderness."*

And without so much as an Amen, they all fell-to.

There let us leave them, five hundred eating like one, tucking-in at their cold viands, licking platter after platter clean, mopping-up the tea and sending the urns empty away, and chewing their celery until the roof resounded with the noise of it.

Behind the scenes, in a smaller room provided with geysers for the making of tea and large sinks for washing-up dirty dishes, a band of earnest workers was toiling at cutting bread at high speed to refill the returned empties from the hall in which the locusts were at work. Pile after pile of bread-and-butter was tipped on the plates which arrived, swept clean, through the hatches. The ammunition was provided by a number of women, armed with fierce and flashing breadknives and who brandished them with machine-like skill and precision. Each lady had brought her own tools, the better to get on with the job. Others continually replenished the tea urns from the steaming, spluttering water-boilers. Now and then, as one of the party left the kitchen for some purpose or another, there would be a brief pause whilst the rest criticised, verbally or by appropriate looks and gestures, her dress, demeanour, speed of work, contribution to the communal labours, or style of headgear — all the women wore hats, by the way — behind her back. Then they would turn-to again.

At length, the backstage garrison was relieved by the sound of scuffling feet — five hundred rising like one from the empty board to return thanks.

This time, the Reverend Partington waits for the piano, which gives out a strident chord, followed by a few voices, which gather reinforcements and momentum as they progress:

"Led and fed, we rise to bless Thee,
Thanks for body, soul replete,
May the whole round world confess Thee,
Kneeling at Thy mercy-seat."

Yes, as you have no doubt guessed, it is a form of grace composed by the great Pogsley himself to fill a long-felt want on such occasions!

Now that the host has been fed, immediate steps are taken to entertain it. The young men of the chapel, therefore, remove their jackets and perform before the eyes of the admiring young ladies, feats of prodigious strength and skill, carrying off the

long, bare-board tables at great speed and depositing them, after
noisily collapsing them, in the storeroom, whilst others dexter-
ously arrange the seats round the edge of the room. The floor
cleared, the hosts of Zion arrayed round the walls, and the
cutters-up now assimilating their share of the banquet in their
own fastness of the kitchens, the minister rises to announce the
pleasures of the evening.

Solos, duets, quartets, improving recitations and a dialogue
with a moral lesson lurking in nearly every line, follow in
rapid succession. The thunders of the rendering of "On
Jordan's Banks" by the choir have just died away when a
muffled commotion occurs at the back of the hall, where a
heavy, elderly man, with a pink, tufted, bald head, white
mutton-chop whiskers, a round, red face and roving blue eyes,
is putting on his hat and coat, greatly to the apparent conster-
nation of a number of spinsters surrounding him. It is Mr
Alderman Harbuttle, senior deacon of the chapel, giving his
annual performance of going home before he has performed
his party-piece. He always does it. It is his perennial act, an
indication that he thinks it high time he headed the game of
follow-my-leader, and if the rest don't agree, he will pack-up
and be off.

"You can't go yet, Mr Harbuttle," twitter the virgins. "We
haven't played 'The Famous Duke of York'."

"Oh, it's getting late. The young folk don't want my old-fashioned games nowadays," says Mr Harbuttle, with jovial coyness.

He would have been surprised if someone had then and
there wished him goodnight. Some of the younger sparks would
gladly have done so, as they wanted to see the last of the elders
and get half-an-hour or so of the rumba or the conga before
turning-out time. But Mr Harbuttle had his following. His
admirers continued their importunities, and finally went to the
extent of noisily, but with due propriety, removing his overcoat
again. It was the signal for a general stampede. Even the ladies

of the kitchen, still wearing their hats, left their retreat to join in.

The game dated from the very beginning of Zion and was initiated and led by Pogsley himself in his day, and his mantle fell on Harbuttle when he passed-on. Rapidly the whole assembly ranged itself behind its leader, in single file. On account of what invariably followed, the young men chose places directly behind the girls of their choice, wives thrust themselves immediately in front of their husbands, unattached spinsters flung themselves into the ranks before helpless bachelors and, now and then, a skittish widower was found prowling in the midst of the members of the Young Ladies' Class, who had massed themselves, tittering, together for protection.

At length all is sorted out, the tussle for positions and possessions subsides, Miss Sleaford, a deaconess, thrusts aside a little widow who has dared to take her reserved place behind Mr Harbuttle. The latter stands ready with his fists squarely in his jacket pockets; the rest each place their hands on the shoulders of the person in front. Many of them will be lowered to waists as the game progresses, but what matter? With a gesture like that of a crowing cock, Miss Sleaford starts the tune:

"Oh, the famous Duke of York,
He had ten thousand men,
He marched them up yon hill,
And he marched them down again.
And when they're up, they're up-up-up,
And when they're down, they're down,
And when they're half-way up yon hill,
They're neither up nor down!"

The chorus is taken up by all the rest and crescendos into a wild roar, the players mark time for a bar or two and then they're off.

The procession is on its way. Tramp, tramp, shuffle, shuffle. About a hundred and fifty of them in a long line; the old folks and children have gone by this, off early to bed. Thrice round the room Mr Harbuttle leads them. He is the best versed in the geography of Zion, its stairways, passages, nooks, crannies and big and little rooms. The old gentleman had given some thought to this game of his. He's going to lead them a dance! So, out of the main assembly hall into the porch, where it is dark on account of the black-out. Round and round, the leader, sure-footed, making his way, the rest following in file, hands on shoulders. Exploring fingers seek responsive waists. There are titters and little screams of mock protest. Here and there, some dried-up reveller tightens her lips in disapproval, whilst wishing the hands firmly clamped on her own bony shoulders would just be a tiny little bit more ardent. Now and then, somebody stumbles, but the long human crocodile seems to have a collective consciousness of its own and falterers and fumbling feet are soon put to rights.

Down two narrow passages, in and out two dark classrooms, to the kitchen and back again, down the narrow steps of the boiler house and up, with the descending column crushing past the ascending one on its way. Mr Harbuttle is at his best tonight. He is like one possessed. He'll show 'em that there's life in the old dog yet! Through the side door and into the open air they stamp, still singing.

> "And when they're up, they're up-up-up,
> And when they're down, they're down,
> And when they're half-way up..."

To the mausoleum of old Pogsley trudges the proud successor of the great man, round the rhododendron bushes twice and off again across the chapel yard, this time to the church. The night is clear, with stars, and the tramping, twittering, canoodling procession goes on its way, silhouetted against the deep blue of the darkness. A kind of frenzy seizes it, as of performers in a ritual dance. The side door of the chapel is unlocked and into the dim, cool building they go, following their leader. A hush falls on the revellers. Gently, firmly they tread. Through the vestibule, down the aisle, past the communion table, its silver ornaments glinting in the shadowy light, and then return down the other aisle. But Mr Harbuttle hasn't finished with them yet. Up the winding stairs to the gallery he pilots them. This is the limit! Nervously the women giggle, and the men seize them with a firmer, protective grip. Miss Sleaford, hands on the great man's shoulders, is tempted to whisper "Enough!" but is held to her course by a strange fascination.

The gallery runs round the whole of the upper walls, but at one end of the chapel it is used as choir pews; the pulpit in front, the organ behind. It is apparent that Mr Harbuttle intends to circumnavigate the gallery and finish up at the side door again.

Tramp, tramp. The singing continues, but pianissimo, now. There mounts upward a soft chant, almost a lamentation.

And when they're down, they're down… The great windows show eerie shadows as the marchers pass them. Somewhere, an overwrought woman bursts into hysterical laughter, which is forthwith muffled as she stuffs her handkerchief between her teeth. The file breaks momentarily, footsteps are heard going in the opposite direction and down the stairs as the sufferer is led off into the fresh air to recover.

Mr Harbuttle is on his way through the choir stalls. He'll give them something to remember him by. He chuckles and then…he vanishes!

Miss Sleaford, marching, rigid and unbending with disapproval behind the leader, feels the great shoulders drop from beneath her clinging fingers and pulls herself up with a jerk. She screams and the whole file halts. There is a great noise of scrimmaging around Miss Sleaford, for Mr Hewston, the church secretary, has needed to tighten his grip on her and throw himself backwards to prevent her from disappearing, too.

There is utter and complete pandemonium in the gallery. A long, drawn-out gasp of horror almost raises the roof. The women scream and groan with terror at whatever unknown thing has happened. In the darkness the commotion, mental and physical, is terrible.

"Somebody strike a light…"

"Don't forget the black-out isn't on here…"

"Has anybody got a torch?"

The members of the Young Ladies' Class are bleating with fear and clutching firmly at the nearest support. Two of them faint. The whole place seems filled with a host of demons. Then, the lights of pocket torches stab the gloom. The women are immediately shepherded outside, whilst a group of men explores the cause of the turmoil.

In the choir pew, about midway along it, is a large trapdoor. This is used on certain choral occasions when a piano is required aloft and, to save struggling up the narrow spiral staircase, it is hoisted through this hole. The trap is found to be open and Mr Harbuttle has stepped down it, never expecting such a pit to open at his feet. Lights are flashed into the void, which terminates on the ground-floor of the chapel behind the pulpit. There lies Mr Harbuttle, unmoving, not emitting a sound.

Along the gallery speeds the throng of men and down the aisle to where the old man sprawls. A number of older women join them and, refusing to be gainsaid or put off, follow in their wake, anxious to render such feminine assistance as may be needed. Momentarily, a circle is formed round the prostrate figure and a dozen or more torches are levelled in its direction. The beams converge and a great gasping groan rises from the whole assembly.

"Don't touch him, don't touch him," says Mr Hewston in an

awful and hushed voice, and gently he bends and himself does what he has forbidden the rest. The body lies face upwards and the eyes are gazing, glazed and open, to the ceiling. The secretary fumbles for the hand and presses his fingers on the pulse.

"Get the police and a doctor," he pants. "Quick, quick. He's... he's...dead."

A fearful commotion occurs again, pent-up emotions break loose and there is a whirlwind of moans, sighs and screams. The beams of the hand-lamps show up with deadly certainty the cause of the tragedy. Buried in the breast of Mr Harbuttle is a knife, its long, horn handle protruding from his heart.

"My bread knife...! I'd know it anywhere," yells one of the ladies to the forefront of the party and then, with a loud bump, for no one has recovered enough from the shock of horror to catch her, she falls inert on the ground.

2

THE TURMOIL SPREADS

Whilst the writhing procession was proceeding on its way to disaster and disintegration, two men had arrived in the schoolroom and, greeting each other, entered into conversation.

One of the two, well past sixty, small, dapper, with a clear, sunburned complexion and a grey moustache, had the fine, intelligent head of a thinker, thatched with silver hair parted to left and to right. His hands were large, well-kept and useful looking. His expression was that of a philosopher whom the world can't startle and who is prepared to take such novelties as it does bring with stoical calm and slightly mocking contempt. His sharp blue eyes flashed beneath bushy white brows. He was Dr Percival, the principal physician in Swarebridge. He had little room in his scheme of things for organised religion and never attended church. Yet, Zion claimed him, for Mrs Percival was president of the Mothers' Union. The doctor, unless detained on business, always drove her to and from worship and social gatherings at the chapel.

There he was, then, waiting for her to return with the rest of the followers of Harbuttle, and spending the time in conversation with another local celebrity who was keeping a similar vigil. The second new arrival was Superintendent Nankivell, chief of the Swarebridge police.

The police officer, too, rarely attended worship at Zion, but, as in the case of the doctor, it claimed him through his wife. In addition, he had been married there; his two daughters were Christened there and attended Sunday School. But the Superintendent liked to keep the congregation at arm's length. A law-abiding, God-fearing lot they were and likely to give him and his force little trouble, but Nankivell was a bit out of his element among them. He liked his glass of beer and they were all TT to a man, or at least professed to be, granting indulgences only in the case of cider and port wine — which they called temperance drinks for some strange reason or other — and the more potent liquors when used medicinally. He also liked to mow his lawn and clip his box hedges on Sundays, which caused such Zionists as passed his garden on these occasions to bow sternly to him and glare with disapproval and, having passed-by, put their heads close together in hissing protests. Nankivell was not a man who ran with the hare and hunted with the hounds. So, he remained a moderate drinker of beer, a Sabbath gardener and he paid little or no homage to Zion, except when collectors for its various "causes" called on him, smiling and forgetful of his sins. Mrs Nankivell did enough at Zion for both of them. She taught the young ladies' class and was in charge of the anniversary catering. On the morrow she hoped to sing in the augmented choir. At the moment, she was relaxing in Harbuttle's crocodile.

Nankivell was a tall, thin man, with long, straight legs, broad shoulders and a general air of clean efficiency and physical power. His face was long and aquiline. A large, hooked nose hung over a firm, pointed chin. He had a high, broad forehead, exaggerated by the fact that he was beginning to go bald and had a promontory of sleek black hair thrusting itself towards his brow in a last desperate effort to stem the retreat. Deep-set, brown eyes and high cheek bones, His face was tanned and his neck red from exposure to the weather, especially the hot Sunday suns of his garden. He was carefully dressed in mufti, with a heavy, blue serge suit, blue soft collar and shirt to match, and well-polished shoes. He was a man of few words and the doctor was doing most of the talking at the time when they entered our tale.

The room is almost deserted. Only the chapel keeper, who is sulking at the thought of so many feet sullying his lovely clean floors, a knot of women too intent on tearing somebody's body and soul apart to join in the frivolities, and some youths and girls who regard follow-my-leader with contempt and are preparing to dance the rumba as soon as the old fogies have gone home; only these are there. From a distance can be heard the revellers, tramping and chanting rhythmically, like devil dancers. They are, by this, just entering the church.

Dr Percival is just telling the Superintendent how he tracked down a typhoid epidemic in 1921 and has just reached the episode where he discovers a workmen's al fresco convenience draining into the Swarebridge and Sticksey Joint Water Board's reservoir, when suddenly the door of the schoolroom is flung open and a ghastly apparition appears.

"Doctor! Doctor! Come at once...ah! Superintendent! Come at once! Mr Harbuttle has been stabbed in the chapel!"

There stands a small, tubby little man, with a face like a full moon made of yellow cheese and a head as bald as a bladder of lard. He usually has red cheeks, but now they seem suffused with bile instead of blood. His eyes protrude dangerously. He is a nobody in Zion. Just Mr Meers, a pleasant, twittering little tittle-tattler, who keeps a small boot shop in the High Street. He has no sooner sounded the alarm than, as if to rob him of the honour of doing it, a struggling mob of women of all shapes and sizes sweep him from the doorway and take up the chorus and, surrounding the doctor and the policeman, bear them off to the chapel, like the receding tide drawing away the litter of the beach.

So violent is the uproar that Albert Hibbs, the aggrieved caretaker, who is normally deaf and impervious to the threats and entreaties of the women of the place, miraculously recovers his hearing and steals to the edge of the milling throng. We next see him in the very thick of the confusion and Superintendent Nankivell is shouting at him louder than all the rest.

"Are the main doors of the church locked, Hibbs?"

"Yes. Never unlocked 'cept for service."

"Then go and lock the yard gates and bring me the key. Nobody is to go out of the buildings until I say so."

This is a wise move and well in keeping with the Superintendent's usual efficiency. A large wall, topped with broken bottles to prevent such as would creep and intrude and climb into the fold of Zion, surrounds the school and chapel and the entrance to the enclosure is effected only by one high, ornamental wrought-iron entrance gate. Such an unathletic lot as the Zionists would be hard put to find one of their number to climb over it. Elsewhere the wall is only broken by the façade of the chapel, with its great double entrance door and the blank wall of the south side of the edifice.

Hibbs picks up his usually shuffling feet, cleaves his way through the melee and before the Superintendent and the doctor can reach the side door of the chapel, he hands the key of the gate to the officer. The two men arrive at the scene of the crime with little more ado. All around them ghostly figures scutter in the gloom, wringing their hands, crying aloud, whispering in corners and forming a confused mass of humanity, like a disordered flock without a shepherd. Superintendent Nankivell hastens to restore order as soon as he perceives, by the light of the flickering torches, what has happened. His voice, quiet and deep like that of a better class cathedral guide, rings round the great building, echoing among the roof beams and arches like the last trump, bringing a great hush over the confused throng.

"Ladies and Gentlemen! I must ask you kindly to adjourn to the schoolroom, where I hope to join you very shortly. Meanwhile, nobody must leave the premises. As a precaution against this, I have had the gates locked. Please don't be alarmed but wait quietly as I ask. I only want your help and co-operation and can assure you that you'll soon be on your ways home if you'll do as I bid. You can do no good here. In fact you'll only impede us by remaining in the church…"

Already a number of people have found urgent reasons for wishing to leave the precincts. Had the doors remained open, nothing would have induced them to depart, but once cribbed and confined, their spirits crave freedom. Nankivell sweeps their objections and excuses aside and joins the doctor, now dusting the knees of his trousers after contact with Hibbs' immaculate floor.

"Dead as a door-nail," says Percival. "Knife through the base of the heart. That'll be the cause of death, although he must have come a pretty cropper falling through that trapdoor from the gallery. The PM will show other injuries, no doubt. But I'd say the knife did the trick. No need to estimate the time of death. These gentlemen will give you that almost to the second."

With a wave of the hand he indicates a small knot of men, still faithfully lighting the scene with flagging torches. They are the secretary and three senior deacons of the church. The group gathered round the corpse reminds one of Rembrandt's School of Anatomy. The tense bodies, anxious faces, the clever profile of the doctor and the heavy black beard of one of the deacons, their figures lost in a background of gloom and long shadows.

"Ah, Mr Dewsbury," says Superintendent Nankivell, addressing the bearded man. "I wonder if you'd mind going to the nearest telephone, asking for the police station and telling

Sergeant Cresswell to come here right away? He's to bring the photographer and usual apparatus for fingerprinting, etcetera. Got that? Thank you."

Mr Dewsbury, a small, very thick-set, hairy man, seems relieved and his ungainly shadow vanishes into the dark body of the building, followed by the Superintendent who lets him out with his key.

* * *

THERE WAS nothing much to be done on the scene of the crime. Even when the constables with their cameras and fingerprint gear arrived heavily on the scene, they found little of use. They took flashlight photographs of the body, but the fact that the chapel had no black-out facilities made every operation difficult. They could not search for fingerprints properly and had to content themselves with waiting until daylight. Let us say here and now that nothing in the way of fingerprints or other tangible clues was found throughout the investigation. The whole place had been so thoroughly trampled and mauled as to make progress in this respect hopeless from the start. The only prints found on the lethal weapon were those of Mrs Butterfield who owned it and had well and truly used it earlier in the day in bread cutting for the feast.

After the knife had been examined, tested and photographed, Mrs Butterfield's own prints were taken. She had recovered from her swoon, but almost developed another and worse kind of fit on being faced with her bloodstained property again. She was an enormous woman, with puffy hands, which she gingerly submitted for the tests. Her face was florid, with fat cheeks, and her chin receded, without any visible neck, into the blue satin dress which concealed a bosom like a featherbed in front and enormous hindquarters behind. She had a little button of a nose, bright black eyes set under a tight, shiny brow and straight dark hair carelessly gathered in a bun under a hat which seemed to rear itself uneasily from her head. She was accompanied by her husband, who hovered solicitously around her, belligerently protective. Together, they looked like Jack Spratt and his wife, for Mr Butterfield was tall and extremely thin. He was dressed in a black suit and wore a combination collar and shirt front drawn together by a black string of a tie. His long, bony hands protruded from sleeves which seemed to have retreated far up his forearms. His head was the shape of a blunt carrot, and as wrinkled. His mouth was a thin line, his nose long and thin, a red, tight-skinned organ, and his ears were all shapes, as though someone had peevishly pulled and twisted them about when he was young. His hair, thin and streaked across his head. Lastly, his face wore a bilious hue, with a touch of colour on the cheekbones and his eyes were blue and dry under next-to-no eyebrows. That was Mr Butterfield, and we have spent so much time over him because he was the treasurer of Zion, the man with the money bags, and the cashier of Pogsley's mills.

"I'd know that knife anywhere," Mrs Butterfield was saying. "It was a wedding present from Joshua's cousin twice removed — not that we expected a wedding present from him. It's a carving knife really, but I always used it for bread. It was such a beautiful cutter…"

"My love! My love!…" protested Joshua Butterfield.

The fat lady had been so carried away with her eulogy of the weapon that she had not realised what she was saying. When brought back to realities by her husband, she wilted visibly and looked round as though seeking a place in which to go over again.

Jack Spratt looked angrily at Nankivell.

"Is there need for any more of this, Superintendent?" he said testily; his voice was like dry, crackling twigs.

"Not at the moment, thanks, Mr Butterfield."

"Come then, my love," said Butterfield to his wife and hitching his short sleeves, he decorously assisted her from the room, in imminent danger of her collapsing on him and annihilating him altogether.

Nankivell, after examining the knives remaining in the kitchen, realised that the killer had made the best choice. Several others would have made excellent weapons of torture, saw-edged, serrated, undulating, long but blunt, keen-pointed but dull-edged. But Mrs B's was the happiest combination for a quick, clean job. Sharp point, firm handle, edge almost razor-like, light and well-balanced for a blow.

In the main hall Sergeant Cresswell and a constable were busy on another task. They had marshalled the assembly into the semblance of a queue and one by one the members passed a table at which the policemen were seated and gave their names. Cresswell had had a brainwave on being given this duty by his chief.

"Ladies and Gentlemen," he had said, blushing furiously, for he was unused to public speaking. "Ladies and Gentlemen, you'll oblige us by forming up in line, h'exactly as you just did behind the, hem — deceased. Then, 'aving taken your respective names, we'll be able to let you go to your 'omes. Those as weren't playing the game of foller-me-leader, be as good as to form-up behind those who were."

One after another, male and female, like the children of Noah passing into the ark, the sons and daughters of Zion gave their names and said whether or not they were Duke-of-Yorking. Cresswell, by a further stroke of genius, for which he later obtained just praise, asked them all the same question.

"Did you keep 'old of the person in front all the time?"

When the answer was in the affirmative, he placed a tick against the name of the person thus cleared of blame. With the exception of six cases and the woman who retired in hysterics, all the members of the crocodile stated they had clung to the person in front throughout and been clung to by the one on their heels. A Deputy Commissioner at Scotland Yard before whom the case came as a matter of interest, in its later stages, described this phenomenon as a *perpetuum mobile* alibi and said that it was unique in their annals. The six who had broken line were temporarily detained and questioned further. We may as well give Sergeant Cresswell's notes on them now and be done with them.

Miss SLEAFORD: *Hands left deceased's shoulders as he fell down trapdoor. Mr Hewston, man behind her, kept his hands on her shoulders. So she's okay.*

Miss CISSIE HORNCASTLE: *Took hands off shoulders of man in front (Mr JC Doane) to adjust hands of man behind (Mr Wilfred Biggins), who, she alleged, was tickling her ribs. Confirmed by both men, but WB states he was doing nothing improper and Miss H was fancying things.*

Mr HENRY TUBBS: *Sneezed on entering open air. Joined up again at once. Confirmed by ladies, back and front. (Mrs E Vivian and Miss G Pomfret.)*

Mr DAVID BUDGE *and Miss* MONICA MITCHELL: *Hesitant at first but forced to confess by other members of procession. They stopped, apparently to kiss in the darkest part of the church porch. Confirmed by Mr R Fryer (in front) and Miss Deborah James (behind). Mr Fryer states that he said "What are you two up to? None of that there here." Miss James says she remonstrated severely with DB and MM, reprimanding them for indecent behaviour in church. Whereupon they joined the file again and behaved properly.*

Mr JOSHUA BUTTERFIELD: *Broke file as church was entered. Said he was annoyed that the game should be led into the sacred edifice. Mrs J*

Butterfield (before) and Miss Jane Tadworth (behind) confirmed. There was a short argument and then Mr B said he'd go on to please them but would protest to Mr Harbuttle when game finished. Several other people confirm hearing argument and temporary halt.

Then followed those who did not join in the game. The knot of gossiping women vociferously gave each other alibis. They also scattered alibis on behalf of Superintendent Nankivell, Dr Percival, all the would-be rumba dancers, a deaf old man who had fallen asleep, and two more old men who refused to go home to their early beds and who, instead, prowled the school room in search of victims on whom to pour streams of reminiscences of by-gone Zion, Swarebridge seventy years ago, and what young people did in 1870.

Cresswell next tackled a very formidable job. He had before him a timetable of the afternoon and evening's events.

2.0 Procession begins.

3.45 Procession ends.

4.10 Tea Starts.

5.15 Everybody finished tea in large hall.

5.15—6.30 Interval for clearing up large hall and to give helpers at tea-tables a chance to get their own teas.

6.30 Concert begins.

8.0 Interval in concert.

8.10 Concert resumed.

8.45 Follow-my-leader begins.

9.05 Approx time of murder as confirmed by Supt Nankivell from time Mr Meers gave alarm.

At the eight-o'clock interval, several mothers with young children — and mostly accompanied by fathers, too — left the place. As Superintendent Nankivell entered the large room he found Cresswell surrounded by a body of enthusiastic female helpers. These pious women, anxious to help and further the ends of justice, were vying with each other in giving the names of those who had departed during the intermission. They were like participants in an auction sale, eager to outdo each other, and fired volley after volley at the sweating officer with the speed of a machine-gun.

"Ladies! Ladies! One at a time, *if you please*," panted Cresswell, lubricating his pencil on the tip of his tongue at such a rate that that organ changed from bright red to dark purple. Some of these daughters of Zion were even prepared to give a character to each of the parties entered in the sergeant's black book and to venture an opinion as to whether or not he or she might be capable of murder. Nankivell, standing on the edge of the milling throng, thought how like a bookie taking bets Cresswell would have looked if only he hadn't been in uniform. He also checked each name hurled at his subordinate's head in his mind's eye. Without exception they were decent, simple family people, leaving a show they were enjoying for the sake of putting the children or grandad to bed early. He could imagine none of them engineering the cunning crime he was investigating. Nankivell was of the opinion that Cresswell's method of approach was simply hunting for a needle in a haystack. There could not possibly be a process of elimination starting from the whole assembly at the feast and whittling away one by one until the limelight fell on the last man. They must begin at the other end. Find the motive and then seek the criminal.

The Superintendent had been thinking hard since the crime had been discovered. He was a kind-hearted man and very loath to begin washing the dirty linen of Zion in public. After all, although his principles didn't coincide with those of the chapel and its congregation, the place held as hostages Mrs Nankivell and his two daughters. Besides, he was on very familiar terms with many of the church members. To most of them he represented the law and the triumph of right over wrong in the secular sphere. But to bring the full machinery of the law into Zion was another matter. Those who watched its workings with equanimity from a distance would prove different when it came to their own doorsteps. What was needed was an impartial outsider, one whom sentiment, past history or friendships would not affect. In other words, this was a Scotland Yard job.

Nankivell made up his mind that he would mention the matter to the Chief Constable of Brentshire by telephone when he got back to the police station. Meanwhile, he was struck by the absence of two of the pillars of the church, the Rev B Augustus Partington and Mr Samuel Wildbore, JP, a senior deacon.

"Where's the minister and Mr Wildbore?" he asked Mr Dewsbury, now standing at his elbow.

"Oh, they've gone to the station to meet Dr Cowslip. He's preaching the anniversary sermons tomorrow...though what's going to happen now, I don't know. As soon as they get back, there is to be an emergency deacons' meeting to decide. It's hardly the occasion for a joyful day of praise after all this..."

Mr Dewsbury seemed annoyed at Mr Harbuttle's getting himself killed on the eve of the great day of the year, especially as Dr Cowslip, a preacher greatly in demand and hard to get, was coming.

"When did they leave for the station?" asked the Superintendent.

"Just before nine. It's nearly half-an-hour to the station, you know. Dr Cowslip's staying with Mr Wildbore over the weekend, so I presume they've gone round to Wildbore's place after meeting the reverend gentleman."

As if in answer to a prayer, the Rev BA Partington, whose initials seemed to mock his fruitless scholastic efforts at London, appeared on the scene. He had no sooner crossed the threshold than he was surrounded by a crowd of ladies, all anxious to be first with the news and to receive comfort from the good man. Under normal circumstances, the sight of so many pretty, flushed faces with helpless, beseeching eyes, plump shoulders and white arms clearly outlined under flimsy yet modest party frocks, and shapely, heaving young bosoms would have gladdened the heart even of the parson. But, as it was, he grew pale, clutched the doorpost and caused all the young women to give rein to the exuberance of their spirits and feelings in noises of sorrow, sympathy, solicitude and pity. From being the spiritual comforter of his flock, Mr Partington was transformed in the twinkling of an eye to the role of principal mourner.

The Rev B Augustus Partington was quite an average parson both in appearance and ability. In spite of his pale face, he looked the part, for he had an ascetic cast of features, which went well on ceremonial occasions. He was a good cricketer, too, which pleased the young men of the place; his sympathetic manner and understanding blue eyes endeared him to the women, especially the unmarried ones. His pale face filled the older ones with a desire to mother him. He was himself married, however, a fact which did not deter his feminine admirers, who made a father-confessor of him, often to his embarrassment. On the occasion of the turmoil in Zion due to

Mr Harbuttle's untimely end, Mrs Partington was away on a visit to her mother, so she took no part in it whatever.

The police were present at the special meeting of deacons and, with their concurrence, it was decided to carry on with the services on the morrow, with suitable references, a change of the hymns from the mood of joy to grief and a general damping-down of anthems and other special items to fit the occasion. Mr Partington, who was due to preach out of town and earn a few extra guineas thereby, thought it best to remain at his own church and, by telephone, was able to substitute for himself a very worthy local preacher from the laymen's panel. The police obliged by getting on the spot very early next day and had finished their technical labours long before the first service was due to start at eleven o'clock.

The only other problem was the Rev Dr Cowslip, who had arrived to preach breezy sermons for the celebrations. The good professor of exegesis proved himself very versatile, however. With a few deft changes, and a new text for each, he converted a morning sermon, based on "Thou hast turned my mourning into dancing," and an evening dissertation on "Make a joyful noise unto the Lord" into masterly discourses which hardly left a dry eye in the place. The chapel was crowded to its very doors at each service, for many gentiles from far afield were impelled by morbid curiosity rather than fervent zeal to visit the place and scores of them were turned away unsatisfied after fruitlessly scuffling for admission.

Late on Saturday night, Superintendent Nankivell telephoned the Chief Constable suggesting the assistance of Scotland Yard. He received a flat refusal.

"What are you botherin' about, Nankivell?" roared the Chief. "You're on your own ground, man. At a job like this no Scotland Yard man can beat you. Don't underestimate your qualities."

The Superintendent explained the delicacy of his task at Zion. The answer was still "NO."

"But I'll tell you what I *will* do. Don't want to be unjust, damn. If you're no nearer solvin' the case in a week's time, we'll send for 'em then. But, as I've said, they'll do no better than you. This is right up your street…damn…"

With this mixed challenge and compliment to put in his pipe and smoke, Nankivell shrugged his shoulders, hung up the receiver and went home to bed.

3

IN MEMORIAM

To see the victim as he actually was before his death shook his native town, we must return a little in time, for a living Harbuttle is much more wholesome than the one stretched on a slab in the Swarebridge morgue.

Samuel Harbuttle and his father, who was then alive, were grocers in Swarebridge when Pogsley raised the lowly village to the honour of a township. Harbuttle, junior, backed the right horse by throwing in his lot with Zion where he became a deacon, secured the custom of the bulk of its congregation and built a grand shop with a chromium-fitted front well in advance of the multiple stores.

The grocer, however, made money in other ways than slapping water into butter or whipping sugar and flour off the scales before they had bumped. As soon as it was whispered that Pogsley might come to Swarebridge, Harbuttle bought land. Not that on which the great mills were built, of course, for Pogsley secured that under another name than his own before anyone knew what was in his mind, but fields behind the village street. Here jerry builders bought plots like wildfire and erupted blotch after blotch of workers' dwellings, which were on their last legs long before the mortgages on them had been repaid. Harbuttle's humble grocery fortune multiplied itself fivefold or more in about three years. This public benefactor became an alderman of the new town council and built himself a large, ugly house on high land on a spot in the borough as remote as possible from the scene of his speculations.

If his capital yielded increase, nature was not very kind to him in other directions, for he was only blessed with one daughter. She made up for much, however, for she was, in her time, by far the prettiest and most sought-after girl in Sware-bridge. Unlike her father, though, she did not cash-in on her endowments. She married a fair-haired assistant in the family grocery shop, greatly to the old man's disgust. Neither father nor daughter spoke to the other for three months after her choice of mate, but the death of Mrs Harbuttle brought them together again and earned for the son-in-law, who boasted the name of Charles Singleton, by the way, a minor partnership and he got back his place at the counter as manager.

Of Mr Harbuttle's collaborator in the procreation of this lovely offspring, we need say little here. She predeceased him by fifteen years. How the pair of them could produce one so fair as Molly Singleton (née Harbuttle) is one of those tantalising problems in which nature baffles man's comprehension. Mrs H in life was a tall, gawky woman with projecting bones. Her lack of physical upholstery, mainly manifest in large "salt-cellars" round the collarbone and a flat chest and spindly arms and shanks, had, until Harbuttle cast longing eyes on the small fortune her father had left her after forty years of losses on a farm, and won it and her, held all amorous advances at arm's length. She was, however, a very worthy woman, a competent housewife and a loyal partner who, in spite of the way in which he bullied and ignored her, left him all she had. It is perhaps enough to say that the "Till we meet again," which Harbuttle sentimentally had chiselled on her headstone, was sufficient to make her turn in her grave at the promise of such a renewal of hell.

For though an alderman and a deacon, Mr Harbuttle was no saint. In late life he was a tall, heavily built, paunchy man, with a round, red, clean-shaven face with side-whiskers, a bald head with a fringe of grey over his rolling bull-neck and a white tuft of fluffy hair over each of his ears. He had a heavy, spreading fleshy nose, a loose, thick-lipped mouth, and small, cunning, pouched grey eyes lost in a network of wrinkles. He had a large, pink, shiny mole right on the top of his head. A man who liked his own way and prone to violent fits of temper if it was long delayed. A non-smoker, teetotaller, not guilty of fornication, Harbuttle's passions were concentrated in a flood of self-assertion, of lusting for power. He stormed and raved at his staff, his tenants, the parson, and anyone else who would let him do so. He boasted of his wealth, health and intelligence and of the inability of any one to take a rise out of him. He relished the humiliation of his rivals for position in Swarebridge and Zion and made enemies wherever he went.

Do not let it be thought that Samuel Harbuttle was universally unpopular, however. He could expand and be generous at times. He paid for the eatables at the anniversary tea party and expected the participants to be grateful. He met the expenses of the annual choir excursion and himself accompanied the singers in a charabanc to distant parts, sitting among the sopranos and entertaining them with heavy witticisms there and back. He enjoyed the company of young, good-looking ladies and not a few of them, in addition to plainer eligibles, would have been quite disposed to tackle the job of being the second Mrs Harbuttle. He lived alone in his great house, with an elderly housekeeper and a maid, and the place seemed ready and waiting for anyone prepared to put up with its owner for the rest of his life, which might not have been too long, seeing that he was seventy-one when he was killed in the chapel.

At each of the anniversary day services, Mr Hewston, the church secretary, made brief reference, among the notices for the week and an appeal for a record collection, to the blow which had befallen their community and to the good life and deeds of their dear brother and deacon. Then, he announced a special church meeting for the following (Monday) evening, the purpose of which was to get together again all those who had attended Saturday's tea party and had then in any way made contact with the deceased. "This meeting is not to discuss church business, but to assist the police in their enquiries and anyone who feels that he or she has any information which might help the officers in any way, is requested kindly to be present," said Mr Hewston, all in one breath and looking like the headmaster he was, demanding that the guilty boy should step in front and take his medicine like a man. There was a collective intake of breath by the congregation, a rustle of hymn-papers and an outburst of whispering as one and another compared notes.

"The collection will now be taken," shouted Mr Hewston challengingly, and left them to it.

The congregation relaxed, sought copper and silver in purses and pockets and the bags went to and fro. The day's offerings were phenomenal and almost created a record, for there were many strangers present and the building was crowded out. Dr Cowslip pleased everyone and many, thinking still of the meeting on the morrow and what they proposed to contribute to it, gave more than they intended. There was also a good catch in coat and trousers buttons, foreign coins, bad half-crowns, bus tickets, and metal and leather washers, such as are placed in offertories by absent-minded churchgoers. On this day, too, the junk included a safety razor blade and a lady's garter. The former was probably given by a simpleton who regularly attended, whilst the latter, it was assumed, had been contributed by some sinner, who, turned from his folly by the eloquence of Cowslip and the fate of Harbuttle, had surrendered the symbol of his sins.

4

MONDAY MORNING

A great depression seemed to set in at Swarebridge on the
Monday after the crime. Apart from the usual grimness
which is reputed to characterise the second day of the week, the
reaction from the events of the two preceding days contributed
further gloom. From the humble chapel keeper, sweeping
together a mass of dust, crumpled hymn sheets, toffee papers
and other oddments, including three handkerchiefs, a shoelace
and a sacrilegious half-smoked cigarette, in the great, cold,
empty church and muttering under his breath as he did so, to
those who had risen to the heights of ecstasy or excitement on
previous days and were now coming-to with a sense of frustra-
tion or anti-climax, everyone entered into a mood of despairing
expectancy. It was as if, knowing that it nursed a murderous
viper in its bosom, Swarebridge realised that it had no means of
bringing it to the light of day and crushing it underfoot. In the
streets, in the shops, behind the closed doors of homes and
among the clattering machines and bale-filled warehouses of
Pogsley's Mills, the same question was asked. "Who in the world
of goodness would want to stab an old buffer like Harbuttle to
death?" Granted he was a pest, even a revolting bully and

swankpot, but that didn't merit a dirty murder in the dark, and in chapel at that! In the matter of solving the crime…well… Nankivell's got a job on. A dark church, filled with folk, capering and chattering. It might be anyone. And as for the people of Zion! Their ears must have burned after what outsiders said about them and their dark revels in their holy place. Such orgies, such goings-on would need a lot of living down!

Superintendent Nankivell had an equable disposition. He did not join in the outbreak of mass depression and disillusionment. He had not been to any of the services the day before. Instead, to the rattle of his lawnmower, which, in his case was a rhythmic aid to thought, he had pondered his problems and, more or less, laid down a provisional plan of campaign. Followed by sympathetic eyes, therefore, he methodically pursued his Monday labours, the first of which was a talk with Harbuttle's housekeeper.

The victim had certainly chosen an ideal spot in which to build his hideous house. It stood on the slope of the highest ground in the district, protected from the winds of winter. It faced the vale of Sware, with its stretch of green, tree-dotted meadows, keeping Swarebridge well out of sight to the left, although from the side windows, anyone with a fancy for tall chimneys and a heterogeneous rash of houses and shops could satisfy himself to the full. As he turned to close the main gate, Nankivell paused to look at the glorious view ahead. The land gently inclined to the river and then, flattening out, spread in fields of brown, green and yellow and parkland as far as the eye could see. On the right, buried in its oaks, chestnuts and sycamores, stood the old manor house, home of the Pogsleys. The son of the benefactor (or malefactor, as you will) of Sware-bridge was now the reigning Pogsley. He had no interest in the mills or in Zion. The former had been sold to a combine; the latter had never appealed to his religious sense since his father had compelled him to attend, and the extent of the family fortune left by the old man by way of endowment had made his son sick at the very thought of the place. Besides, he was known to keep a mistress in London, and felt uncomfortable under the virtuous eyes of the congregation.

The late Alderman Harbuttle's residence boasted the name of "Pisgah." It stood just off the main road along which were ranged the other houses of the town's dignitaries, the town clerk, the borough treasurer, two or three solicitors, business-men, and the like. The Alderman in instructing his architect, was determined to outdo the lot of them in splendour. The result was a towering, spreading, ostentatious edifice, sprouting turrets and serrations and more like a factory than a place of human habitation. Nankivell made clicking noises with his tongue as he approached it. The place seemed to shriek its own advertisement. "Get a load of me! I'll show 'em that when 'Arbuttle builds, he builds somethin' proper!"

The inside was almost as bad as the outside. It smelled musty, short of air, to start with, as though all the windows had remained closed from the day it was built. The atmosphere in the hall bore suggestions of dust, damp and decaying paper, exotic pot-plants from an unseen conservatory, and tainted meat from distant kitchens. The furniture looked as if it had been moved in from a smaller house and then augmented from sale rooms and piecemeal purchases from other sources. It was ponderous and out-of-date. The pictures, mainly oil colours and execrable and heavy, added to the general effect of bumptious ignorance. Harbuttle had had no woman about him, other than servants, when he built and fitted-out his Pisgah, and, instead of knocking his neighbours cold with envy, he made a fool of himself and a monstrosity of his abode.

Harbuttle's housekeeper was Mrs Merchant, a straight-backed, efficient looking, faded little woman of sixty or there-abouts. She was roaming about the place in a daze when

Nankivell arrived. She was expecting the body from the morgue at any time, she said. Her sitting room, to which she conducted the Superintendent, was simply furnished and held at least one comfortable armchair in which she bade him be seated.

"I don't want to bother you at a time like this, Mrs Merchant," began the officer when they had settled themselves, "but the sooner we get all the information we can, the better. We want to lay the murderer by the heels as quickly as possible, don't we?"

"Yes. I suppose we do. What can I do to help?"

"I'm interested in what Mr Harbuttle was doing before his death. Anything outstanding, anything interesting, which might throw some light on why someone should bear him a grudge enough to want him out of the way. Had he any enemies that you can think of, Mrs Merchant?"

"Well, not enemies who'd want to do him bodily harm. He'd plenty who disliked him and would have liked to belittle him, but that's a long way behind wanting to kill him, isn't it? He was a hot-tempered man, was the master, and don't I know it, but he never meddled in the housework, so I could tolerate him. You've only to look at the reports of the local council meetings to see how quarrelsome he was, though, and proud of it, too, if you ask me."

Nankivell got the impression that the woman bore her late master no love and only put up with him because hers was a good job. Perhaps, too, she had carried in her heart that strange hope, so often cherished by many of her kind, that luck would one day smile on her and she'd become mistress of the place in her own right and had been thwarted somehow.

"What did Mr Harbuttle do with his time since he gave up active interest in the shop?"

"There were the council meetings. He was still keen on local politics. After breakfast, he went every day, except Sunday, which he mainly spent at chapel, to the Constitutional Club in the town. He'd meet his friends there, read the daily papers and sometimes he'd boast they'd arranged affairs beforehand ready for the next council meeting. He strolled about the streets, too. I've often seen him when I've been shopping. He was interested in the life of the town. Often meddled in it and got himself unpopular with his suggestions and criticising what didn't really concern him. After lunch, he'd have a nap and then take a stroll along the road, or else sit at the window with his field-glasses, watching the road and the country and what was going on in them."

"Yes? And then...?"

"After tea, he'd always some meeting or other. Chapel or local town council. Often, he'd have a meeting in the afternoon, too. He was fully occupied always. A busy man."

The woman seemed disgruntled and Nankivell began to probe as to its cause.

"Did you say you got on well with your master?"

"Yes, most times. He'd fly up in tempers sometimes and then be sorry and soft-soaping after it, but I just used to take no heed of his tempers or his soft-soap. He'd apologise with one breath and get in a rage again with the next, so I let it go in one ear and out of the other. All things considered, the job was a good one; I was well paid, got my own way in things concerning me and he said he'd remember me in his will and see me comfortable. I've been with him since his wife died. I'll miss him..."

Tears ran down Mrs Merchant's cheeks. She dried them with a wet handkerchief and sniffed; then she composed her face again.

"Have you had any troubles recently with your late employer?"

"What do you mean?"

The woman eyed him aggressively.

"What I say. Has anything unusual occurred of late?"

"I might as well tell you then. It's over and done with now. He was thinking of getting married again."

So that was Mrs Merchant's grievance!

"Yes? To whom?"

"I don't know. He didn't tell me. All he said was, 'If I was to get married again, would you stay on here, Mrs Merchant? I'd like you to carry on. The new Mrs Harbuttle wouldn't have to do housework.' 'That depends on who it is,' I says, taken aback like. I wanted to think it over, but if it meant little change, I felt I'd be as well staying-on at my time of life than trying to get another job. But I'd my doubts as to whether it would work. It seldom does. You can't have two mistresses in a kitchen, and I've been in charge at Pisgah too long to knuckle-under to another woman. I decided I'd give it a trial and then pack my things and go if it didn't suit."

"Did Mr Harbuttle say whom he intended marrying?"

"No. As far as I could guess, he'd not asked her, but was making quite sure that all was right beforehand. Perhaps he thought it would be nice if he could tell her she needn't soil her hands with housework. Old men get like that when they marry again, especially if it's a young un."

"So he *did* say she was a young lady?"

"Oh, yes. Smiled funny and awkward like; awful it looked in a man like him. 'She's a nice girl I've got my eye on and she's young,' he says. 'I'm going to surprise some of them.'"

"He mentioned no names?"

"No. He was a close one when he set out that way. Thought it was clever, no doubt. Probably it was somebody at the chapel who'd been flattering him. There's a lot down there who'd jump at the first that offered, young or old."

"Yes. That's very useful, and I'll bear it in mind. Had he many visitors at the house?"

"No. He kept pretty much to himself. But, of course, he was nearly always out. His daughter and son-in-law, with the two

41

children, used to come up after Sunday School and stay to tea some Sundays."

"Did they get on well?"

"Oh, yes. The old man was fond of the children and proud of them. His daughter wasn't what you'd call the loving sort. She was her mother's girl from what I can gather. He didn't seem to like Mr Singleton. Always trying to show him up, he was. That can be understood, can't it, seeing that he never really approved the marriage? He practically gave the shop to them when he retired from business, but he was always grumbling about how his son-in-law ran the place, losing customers to the new multiple stores, buying badly and the like. I have heard him say that he'd given them the business and they'd better make a go of it, as he wasn't putting any more money in it."

"I don't suppose his daughter knew about this proposed second marriage, eh, Mrs Merchant?"

"Not that I'd know of. He made me swear to say nothing and if I know him, he'd never have told anybody else until whoever it was had said Yes. He was far too proud to risk being publicly laughed at if she'd said No."

"So, you can't throw any light on what might have caused him to be murdered?"

"No, I can't. The whole thing's bewildering to me. I don't know what to think of it. I only hope he's kept his promise and not forgotten me in his will."

"Who were his executors, do you know?"

"Mr Roebuck, the solicitor, and the bank, I think. When he made his will, the manager and Mr Roebuck called here, and I had to get the maid and gardener to sign as witnesses. I wasn't allowed to see what was in it, of course."

"Well, I'll be calling again later with Mr Roebuck to go through Mr Harbuttle's private papers and the like, so don't touch anything, will you?"

"As if I would!" replied the woman with animation. "You can

have a look now if you want. Of course, his desk is locked and he'd the only key."

"No. The key is at the police station and we'll attend to that in due course. He'd not received any letters or such to disturb him?"

"No. I always brought them to him after the postman called. He'd open them over breakfast. If anything had come to upset him, he'd have left his meal untouched. I've known him do that in times past."

"You were saying something about his looking round with binoculars, Mrs Merchant. Are these the glasses?"

Nankivell picked up a pair of good racing glasses, which were lying, apparently as the old man had last left them, on the window ledge.

"Yes. He seemed to get a lot of pleasure watching things. Especially of late."

"Anything in particular?"

"Not that I'd know of. He seemed a bit excited now and then. Perhaps he'd seen a good-looking girl on the road."

"He was that way inclined, eh?"

"No. No different from other men."

Evidently the marriage question had given Mrs Merchant cause for bitterness.

Nankivell picked up the binoculars and focused them on the broad view, the Canaan so often surveyed by the dead patriarch from his Pisgah.

The scene was magnificent under the morning sun. On the horizon, dim hills and an indefinite line of trees. Then, straight ahead, the oaks of Buckleigh Manor park, with Whitestone Ring, an old earthwork surrounded by a fringe of trees, to the left. There was a searchlight battery on The Ring and Nankivell could make out the soldiers, some cleaning the huge light, others about their business of tidying their camp, preparing meals, or tuning-up the generating plant. The forms of two sentries could be plainly seen. They, too, were busy with binoculars, passing the time watching friendly planes in the sky or picking out landmarks. The left-hand view from the window just missed the town. Nearer, in the vale of Sware, were dotted three farms. To the right, Vale Farm, to the left Park Farm and, midway, Doyle's. The latter was a shabby affair; the other two trim and neat. Nankivell could make out and recognise figures moving among the farm buildings of each. Labourers cleaning out the cowsheds and stables; women about their kitchen tasks, carrying potatoes or emptying slops on the manure heaps in the farmyards.

Then, in the foreground came the main road leading to Swarebridge, a ribbon of black and white tar and flints. Villas, cottages and bungalows were strewn in single file along it, their roofs of many colours, flamboyant, the shoddy work of gimcrack builders.

"Hm," said Nankivell, lowering the glasses and screwing up his eyes from strain. "Interesting. A pretty wide range of vision, eh?"

In his keen mind he had photographed and filed that scene for future reference. Perhaps the old man had stumbled on something going on in an isolated spot of that vast expanse, meddled, and sealed his own fate. A huge field of investigation, too. It might be a soldier in the camp, a stranger on the road, an intruder in the fields, an occupant or an interloper in any one of the string of houses below!

Nankivell sighed, hitched up his belt, bade Mrs Merchant goodbye, and thanked her. In the quiet lane between Pisgah and the high road, he lit a cigarette and slowed his pace. As a rule, he did not countenance smoking in uniform by himself or his men, but today he felt he needed the solace of tobacco. In his progress downhill he was faced by the scene he had contemplated from the window above and its enormous possibilities and challenge depressed him. The weight of Monday descended on his spirits.

He puffed and pondered, seeking a starting point in vain. Then, he turned the bend and Swarebridge with its buildings, chimneys and teeming life came in view. In a remote corner on the edge of it, Nankivell could make out his own house and beside it, the flat expanse of lawn which was his pride. Smiling again, he flung away his cigarette, decided that it was a meal he needed, and hastened his steps homewards.

5

PILLARS OF ZION

Almost all the well-to-do people of Swarebridge live within a stone's throw of Pisgah. Solicitors, bank managers, municipal big-wigs, retired tradesmen and the rest have congregated there like a flock of superior sheep, for it is to windward of the town and the prevailing winds are clean when they arrive there on their way to pick up the dirt and smoke of the factories and deposit it over the eastern side, known as downtown.

But it must not be thought that all the pillars of Swarebridge and Zion are perched on the hillside jostling with Harbuttle to overlook his Canaan. We must not forget those whose daily toil, lack of private means of conveyance or personal tastes compel them to live downtown. Such are, for example, Superintendent Nankivell; his assistant, Inspector Patchett, whose semi-detached residences are handy for the police station in the High Street; the Rev Partington, whose manse overlooks the chapel; and such shopkeepers as Mr William Burt, prosperous butcher; Miss Sleaford, of the wool shop, and Mr Hewston, the school-master, who lives opposite the new central school of which he is

the headmaster. There is Mr Plumpton, too, the ironmonger…
But we could go on enumerating these worthy downtowners
like threading beads on a string, but the ones we have
mentioned are the larger, brighter ornaments and we need not
bother ourselves with the smaller fry just at present.

As Nankivell made his way homewards, he passed the new
school from which Mr Hewston was emerging wrapped in
gloomy thought. The place was a large, two-storeyed, red-brick
edifice, with a low wall topped with wrought-iron railing
enclosing it. There was a barren asphalted playground for each
sex and along one side of each quadrangle ran a series of small
garden plots, the school's contributions to the dig-for-victory
effort. From these beds sprang all kinds of strange, gaunt
growths, such as bare stalks stripped of all their brussel sprouts,
lettuce plants grown high, flowering and gone to seed, and
anaemic-looking broccoli which appeared to have been abandoned in disgust. A few stray children, who seemed unwilling to
go home, dawdled about the playgrounds, and Mr Hewston,
suddenly awaking from his brooding, began to scutter round
like a demented sheepdog, gathering the stragglers together and
with scooping gestures of the hands urging them to the pedes-
trian crossing before the main gate. He observed the Superintendent and gave him a grave greeting.

Mr Hewston is a tall, broad-shouldered, big-boned man with
large hands and feet. He has small, beady, black eyes, high
cheekbones and a huge roman nose, which has earned him the
nickname of Conky from successive generations of his pupils.
His upper lip is hidden by a massive drooping moustache,
which, unlike his straight, thinning, black hair, is sandy; his
lower lip is a bit too loose and fleshy. He is forty-eight and a
bachelor and his face is pale, with a pimple here and there on his
chin and the back of his neck. Mr Hewston suffers from chronic
intestinal torpor, which makes him peevish and physically

inclined to lethargy. His mind, however, is active and constantly at war with his slothful body. This causes Conky to indulge in spurts of enforced activity as the spirit flogs the flesh. During such periods of flagellation he is a fury, spurring on the diggers to their gardening, urging on the recalcitrant with a cane, starting new systems of scholarship and burdening his staff with fresh duties. Then he will relapse, leaving a trail of weeds and untended cabbages in the allotments, a crowd of puzzled idlers and malefactors unpunished, and a lot of under-teachers perplexed as to where they are or what they're doing.

Nankivell approached Hewston.

"Morning, Mr Hewston. I'm glad I've met you. I'm wanting to see you as soon as possible about Saturday night's events and what you, as a man on the spot, can tell me of 'em…"

"We can't talk here, Superintendent," replied Hewston vaguely. "Let's get lunch over and then, if you care to, call at the school about two o'clock and let's chat it out. That do?"

They parted without more ado, for they were not fond of each other. On two or three occasions, it had been as much as Nankivell could do to keep parents of boys who had probably deserved a thrashing but received too much of it, from assaulting Hewston, or dragging him to court. Nankivell, in turn, had sent his girls to a private school in the town and the affronted central schoolmaster had given him a bad mark for it.

Nankivell called at the police station on his way. There he found Dr Percival in conference with Inspector Patchett. In his capacity as police surgeon, the little, grey-haired man had just finished probing the secrets of the deceased Harbuttle's anatomy. Nankivell was just in time to hear his tale.

"Mornin', Nankivell," said the doctor, who was sitting on the edge of the Inspector's desk, his hat on the back of his head and his pipe between his teeth. "I'm just tellin' Patchett that old Harbuttle wouldn't have lasted long. So, whoever's cut him off long past his prime has beaten natural causes to the post by about two years. Arteries shockin'! Heading for a stroke any time!"

Patchett grinned as though listening to some comic entertainment. He was a pleasant, bulky, red-faced officer from Sussex and his sense of humour leaned to the dry, caustic type in which Dr Percival was an expert. He rose deferentially to meet his chief.

"The coroner's officer phoned to say tomorrow's okay for the inquest, sir. Meanwhile, here's the doctor's report."

He handed Nankivell a closely written document, which the Superintendent placed in his pocket. After lunch would be a better time for perusing the grisly details of the corpse and how Harbuttle had been converted into it.

"Mrs Butterfield's bread knife did the job properly," went on Percival. "So did whoever used it. A straight, clean stroke carefully placed, which cut dead into the heart. It needed a strong arm and what I'd call an expert blow..."

"In what way?" interposed Nankivell.

"Well...no fumbling. You know how trained assassins work... Corsican brothers, Mafia and all that... A swift, precise stab and the victim's dead without a sound except a last gasp. And by the way, if your witnesses, if you can call 'em such, seein' that it was all done in the dark, didn't see any lights used by the murderer to guide him, don't be dismayed. He'd another way. Before we stripped the old chap, we played, as usual, at reconstructin' the blow. Harbuttle fell down the hole before he knew what was happenin' and it was large enough for him to slip through entirely without touching the edges. I reckon he'd drop face downwards, probably crouching a bit, and dazed and surprised. The murderer, who'd been waitin' there, was on him and struck at once. He just gripped and turned the old chap over and stabbed him like this... Kneel down on the floor, man, and let's put you out of your misery..."

And Percival leapt from the table and forced Patchett into a posture which reminded the Inspector of Position No 3 of his daily exercises. Body horizontal on the ground, face downwards, supported on the toes and by the palms of the hands. Instead of straightening the arms and raising the body, however, Patchett, smiling and scarlet to the roots of his hair, surrendered himself to the surgeon, who, hat still on the back of his head, seized him swiftly at the root of the neck, pulled his head and chest backwards and, with a quick cross-blow, caught him a smart tap over the left breast.

"Not quite as comic or gymnastic as that," said the doctor, helping the grinning Patchett to his feet, "but that's the idea as I see it. As to how he found the spot in the dark... Well, Patchett's tunic prevented our including that in the show, but actually the knife cut clean through the top, inner corner of the old chap's upper waistcoat pocket. In other words, the killer just had to hook his free finger there and he was on the exact spot for a deadly stroke. He'd evidently given his victim the once-over beforehand."

"Could have been done without a light, then?" said Nankivell.

"Yes, I'd say so, although the operator might have cut his fingers if he wasn't careful. The type of blow cuts out women, weaklings and fumblers, which still leaves you with hundreds to choose from. Sorry I can't help you any further. I'll be at the inquest to say my piece..."

* * *

AFTER LUNCH, the Superintendent, who had a good half-hour to spare before calling at the school, decided to visit Miss Sleaford at her wool shop and, in a quiet interview, get a first-hand account of how Mr Harbuttle vanished from beneath her very nose to meet his untimely end.

Miss Sleaford's shop is in the High Street and we may as well accompany Nankivell, and thus familiarise ourselves with the heart of the town. Gracious old and hideous new mingle indiscriminately in the main shopping thoroughfare. First, we come to the principal picture-house, sleek, straight concrete like a relic of the Wembley Exhibition with a café included. There is a space for a car park, created by pulling down a sweet little Georgian house once occupied by the only doctor. Next, a structure which caused a great commotion in Swarebridge when it was erected. A multiple-tailors' place, all chromium and imitation marble, which replaced the Old Bridge Hotel, a coaching-inn with centuries of tradition behind it for good food, comfortable beds, cheerful hospitality and pretty serving wenches. There was even a ghost. All were swept away by the tailors, but not without a struggle, inspired by the local society for the protection of historic monuments and the like. But the enthusiasts cried in the wilderness. What can you do when the Mayor, Aldermen and most of the corporation hold shares in the concern you're fighting? Down came "The Bridge" and up went the multiple suits. Not that the tailors were much to blame. The man who bought the hotel right under the noses of local worthies, including Harbuttle, who intended to do just the same thing as the purchaser if they could get it, was open to the highest offer. The tailors topped the bidding.

Now, we pick our way through queues of women, strained, eager, some of them cantankerous, outside the shops of the greengrocer, Mr Figg, and the pastry cook, Mr Meister. The greengrocer's has one window devoted to fish and the other to oranges and roots. There is little left in the fish side, but swarms of blue-bottles and cods' heads; the other side is causing a local riot. Mr Meister is a Swiss confectioner, who, in the last war, had his shop windows broken three times and had to flee to a country retreat on account of his name. This time, however, he is very popular, for he still sells stuff which tastes pre-war. He constantly recites the details of what the Swiss will do to the Germans (he calls them "Chermans") and Italians if they dare to violate his own land. He provided the cakes and loaves for the fatal feast at Zion, and we shall meet him later.

Mr William Burt is at the door of his butcher's shop as we pass. It is a clean, prosperous one with plenty of space but little meat, for Monday is an off day in the trade. He has one of the bulldogs he breeds snoozing at his side in the doorway, and the ugly, friendly animal opens one eye and then closes it again.

"Hullo, Nankivell," booms Burt, a tall, heavy, red-faced, shifty-eyed man of sixty or thereabouts, who has made a lot of money and is a town councillor. His head is bald, his brow beetling and he looks as if he lives on a diet of flesh and blood from the shop, which results in violent sanguinary passions and emotions. "Hullo, Nankivell. Things began to happen at Zion after I left on Saturday. Keep you chaps busy. Give you something to do, instead of fining people for black-out offences."

Mr Burt is bitter because his fellow justices of the peace charged him two pounds last week for showing a naked light in his kennels.

Nankivell remains unperturbed and gives the butcher a civil good day.

"You were at the gathering then, Mr Burt?" he asks calmly.

"Oh, I just went along to cut up the meat, as I generally do. Although I say it myself, nobody in this town can make a pound of ham go further than I can."

Which is quite true. One would expect the main butcher of the place to be an expert slicer. Until earlier this year, Mr Burt was a pillar of Zion, a deacon and a vociferous member of its councils. He resigned with a grievance, however. His daughter, Matilda, had, to please her father, spent long unhappy years learning the organ. She had made little progress, however, but her parent thought she was at least good enough to preside over the large instrument at Zion, and when, in May, the resident organist had resigned and left the town to officiate at the keyboard of a London cinema, her father had insisted on Tilly making application for the job, which he was sure she'd get.

Others thought differently, however. Among them was Harbuttle, of course. Mr William Henry Jelliby, Mus Bac, FRCO, won the day. After a stormy meeting, Mr Burt withdrew in a huff, cut off Zion with a shilling, resigned his church offices and took his family away from worship. Tilly, the unwilling cause of the feud, was fearfully upset. All her friends and the man she fancied attended Zion, and she longed to get back. Knowing that father had an eye for a pretty girl, she at length persuaded the best-looking members of the Young Ladies' Class to form a deputation and plead for the butcher's attendance at the anniversary revels. Under a bombardment of flashing eyes, arch looks, pleas, persuasions and fluttering bosoms, the butcher had capitulated, but to save his face, had stipulated that he'd only attend the tea party to officiate at the cutting-up of the hams. The lovely deputation, satisfied that the thin end of the wedge had been inserted, retired laughing and chattering from the spacious living-quarters over the shop, leaving the butcher feeling very pleased with himself and short-tempered with his wife, who had not stood up well to time and her husband's bullying, and was plain and shapeless.

Nankivell knows all about this but pretends he doesn't. Mr Burt hems and haws.

"The chapel sent a deputation with an apology for the shockin' way they treated me and the family. So I decided to bury the 'atchet. But on my own terms, mind you, on my own terms. Nobody at Zion's goin' to tell me what I must do…"

"Glad to hear the trouble's over," says Nankivell tactfully and extricates himself skilfully. He hasn't all day to listen to the boasting of the overbearing meat salesman.

Now comes perhaps the best part of Swarebridge's main

street. Four very old shops with bow windows and the old-fashioned glass which seems so shiny and iridescent in its small
panes and with the blobs of bottle-glass to set it off. The
chemist's shop; a sweets and tobacco stores with a crowd
milling round the door, for fresh supplies have just arrived; an
iron-mongery emporium kept by Mr Plumpton and which is
overflowing with women who have heard that kitchen shovels
are about to be rationed and are anxious to lay-in stocks; and,
finally, Miss Sleaford's wool shop, right opposite the heavy
portals of the Constitutional Club, the flag of which flies at half-
mast for Harbuttle. To the left as you enter the wool shop,
stands the Jubilee Clock, a hideous erection like an elongated
wedding cake, which once upon a time, struck the quarters for
twenty-four hours in the day. Now it only strikes between 8 am
and 10 pm, thanks to a deputation of sleepless commercial travellers who frequented The White Lion, right under the very
tower itself, and who suffered from a species of chiming
insomnia every time they came to Swarebridge.

The clock is just striking 1.15 as Nankivell enters Miss
Sleaford's. A bell hanging from a spring over the door jangles as
he opens it, and the owner of the shop pops out from a
curtained opening at the back like Mrs Noah hastily
announcing the imminence of rain. She rushes straight to the
counter as though propelled by some unseen mechanical
contraption. In these days of knitting for the Forces she is a very
important part of the national effort and feels the responsibility
of it. She pulls up with a jerk in front of Nankivell, raises her
head and stares at him as though unable to believe her eyes. Are
the police starting knitting, too? she thinks. Then the awful
purport of the visit dawns on her. She utters a stifled little
squeal and clutches the edge of the counter as if about to swoon.
Then, she pulls herself together like one who knows where her
duty lies.

"Good afternoon, Superintendent," she says with dignity. "Will you come through…?"

And she leads Nankivell into her private quarters behind the shop, which are sacrosanct except to the favoured few.

6

THE CHALLENGE AT THE CLUB

M iss Sleaford's shop reminded Nankivell of some fantastic kind of air-raid shelter. The walls on two sides of it were covered from floor to ceiling with shelves heaped with wool in brown and white paper packages like neat little sandbags. The third side was decorated with balls, skeins and hanks of knitting-wool in many different colours like spaghetti dyed for a grotesque carnival. There were smaller bundles and bobbins of the same material, silk, and linen threads on the counter with masses of buttons and tapes. A species of what-not in front of the counter held knitting and needlework magazines of all types, displaying on their covers anything from pullovers and jumpers to doilies and tea-cosies. At the bottom of this pile were decently concealed pictorial details of more intimate articles of feminine attire with full particulars of how to make them from components cunningly hidden here and there in Miss Sleaford's shop.

Nankivell, at the owner's invitation, steered his way through this mass of raw products of feminine industry and allure and entered the private quarters behind. Impossible to describe this sanctum! An inventory would fill many volumes. It was chock full of every kind of furniture and appendage. Sofas and "easy" chairs of stiff and forbidding by-gone patterns, occasional tables, hassocks, footstools, in hopeless confusion. The furniture draped in antimacassars and covers of wool and lace, bedecked with ribbons. Every available ledge and shelf littered with ornaments and knickknacks. Walls covered with photographs in frames of seashells, passe-partout and poker worked wood. Little cards bearing trite, bright sayings or bits of jingling rhymes in the spaces between the portraits and snapshots, and over the fireplace two framed and choice jewels of wisdom. "DON'T WORRY: IT MAY NEVER HAPPEN." "TOMORROW NEVER COMES."

A bright fire was burning. The room was stuffy, and the remains of a neat and simple meal were still on the table.

"You'll excuse the disorder, Superintendent, won't you?" said Miss Sleaford, her cheeks flushed with excitement. "I didn't expect you. Will you have a cup of tea?"

Nankivell said he wouldn't, thank you. She scuttered and twittered about, removing and concealing packets and bundles and clearing a space for action. She bade her visitor be seated and he gingerly lowered himself on a horsehair couch, which felt like an unshaven chin and the hairs of which pierced even the stout cloth of his regulation trousers and tickled the skin beneath. A loose cover embroidered with a galleon in full sail on a sea of peacock-blue slid to the floor with a hiss and a muffled thud.

Miss Gertrude Sleaford was an uncertain fifty-five and did not believe in dressing-up her mutton as lamb. She was an honest, truthful person and did her best to live up to the simple faith she had always held. Her mother had built up and left her a prosperous little business after the death of Sleaford *père*, when Gertrude was seven. Photographs of father and mother looked down from each side of the over-mantel. On the mantelpiece between them stood a faded snapshot of a soldier dressed in the old-fashioned cut of uniform of 1916. He was lost in France and constituted Miss Sleaford's one romance. She was a very nice and capable little woman, somewhat prim from long spinster-hood and apt to fuss around a bit, but she would have made him a good wife had things gone well.

Fundamentally, Miss Sleaford was sound; sound in heart and according to those who *knew* at Zion, sound in doctrine. She gave away as much as she could spare, surreptitiously, to the needy. She was of medium build, thin, angular and as trim and clean as a she-cat. She had an old-fashioned figure and, although she had used no contrivance to assist nature since her teens, she somehow gave the impression of wearing a bustle; just a suggestion of it! Her face was set in patient lines with loose, soft skin, netted with tiny wrinkles, but healthy-looking. Small, sharp nose and large brown eyes. Cranford, alas, has passed; Miss Sleaford would have fitted in there quite nicely and been thought one of the moderns at that!

She was a lady deacon of Zion and worked hard at the job both in the spirit and in the flesh. Somehow, she and Harbuttle had through the years grown into partners in committees and church councils and in her own mind Miss Sleaford had estab-lished proprietary if platonic rights to him in that sphere. She flattered herself that she had a good and restraining influence over him, which was quite true. The members of the inner courts of Zion in which the pair of them sat, recognised this power of restraint which she exercised and relied on her. She called herself to herself, dear Mr Harbuttle's sister-in-God. Perhaps at the back of her mind she harboured a fond hope of improving the relationship one day. Who knows? But behind all her visions of possible matrimony — and there had been a few — was the comfort of the photo on the mantelpiece. She had loved and lost him and, come what may, there was still consola-tion in that past romance. He had been a soldier billeted in Swarebridge in 1915. He met her at the Saturday evening concerts at the Sunday School. She had been worth looking at then. So he took her home and afterwards met her, took her for walks along the path by the Sware, and kissed her a time or two. Then off to another place and, unknown to Miss Sleaford, another girl. A few letters which she still kept somewhere safe among a welter of odds and ends and a newspaper cutting telling that he was missing. He turned up after the armistice, but not at Swarebridge. In the heart of Miss Sleaford was enshrined through twenty lonely years, a young man who, still alive and now gross and fat, keeps a little pub in the Walworth Road and beats up his wife every Saturday night.

But here is Nankivell, sitting on the couch and fidgeting for a comfortable place among its potent, bulging springs and whiskery hide.

Miss Sleaford sat upright in an uncomfortable oak elbow-chair, carved and contorted with scrolls, knops and bulges. Eager and questioning, she looked at her visitor.

"Well, Miss Sleaford, this is a sad business. Most distressing for you, I'm sure," said Nankivell.

She sniffed, as if about to burst into tears and then thought better of it.

"He oughtn't to have gone into the church — he really oughtn't. It seems like a judgment, Superintendent," she whispered. Evidently, she hadn't got over the sacrilege.

"Now. Can you throw any light on why he should have deviated from his usual sedate game? Surely, he never led his followers such a dance before."

"I can't fathom it at all, except that he seemed all excited that night. I've never seen him so pleased with himself. I can't think what had possessed him. He was bubbling over with joy and I did hear him say to himself once, 'I'll show them whether I can cut a dash or not.' Whom he meant I cannot say. And when I remonstrated with him as he entered the church, he just turned his head and said over his shoulder, 'Oh, be quiet, Gertie...' —

Gertie, if you please, a form of my name I greatly dislike, and which no one at the chapel would think of using — 'Oh, be quiet, Gertie. You are like a prim old hen. We must have our *bit of fun* for once.' I almost broke from the ranks at that. I was so shocked and hurt. But thinking that if I, as second in the file, gave up, the whole would be spoiled and poor Mr Harbuttle humiliated, I remained."

Miss Sleaford paused to take breath and to reinvigorate herself by a sniff at a large smelling-bottle which she unearthed from some part of her clothing.

"So you can't think of anything which might help me in my search for the murderer?"

The little lady almost screamed at the word and inhaled deeply at her bottle again, surrounding herself with ammoniacal fumes. She pursed her lips, looked thoughtful and hesitant, then:

"Perhaps I *could* tell you what was *said*, Mr Nankivell, but I quite discounted it. Quite. Seeing where it came from, I mean. I don't believe it at all. Mr Harbuttle, such a model of *right* behaviour, couldn't do such a thing..."

"Yes?" chimed-in the Superintendent, more to bring Miss Sleaford back to earth than anything else, for she seemed to be holding a conversation with her conscience.

"Well, after the evening service on Sunday, I passed a small group of people in the porch at chapel. They included those awful Briggs. You know, he's an estate agent and he *drinks*. They rarely attend church, although they *pretend* to belong to the place. Mr Briggs and his wife were talking to some strangers. They'd all come out of curiosity, I'm sure, and I distinctly heard Mr Briggs say to the rest, 'If you ask me, he led them into the chapel for a *bet*.'"

She almost screamed the last word and her eyelids fluttered like aspen leaves in a wind.

"A bet? Surely not!" said Nankivell.

"I'm so glad you don't believe it, Superintendent. That's what the awful man said. The others were incredulous, too, as well they might be. Why, Mr Harbuttle wouldn't even tolerate raffling and Christmas draws at Zion, not to mention *betting*. But Briggs insisted. 'I heard him at the club, I tell you,' he kept saying. I passed-on, lest I should forget myself and rebuke the man, and be sorry for my outburst afterwards. Speaking evil of the dead, who can't defend themselves!"

She dried the corners of her eyes meticulously and blinked rapidly again.

"I wouldn't worry about it, Miss Sleaford," said Nankivell. "These common fellows will have their vulgar jokes, you know."

But he made a mental note to pursue this betting line more closely later.

"Did you see any lights down the hole in the floor after Mr Harbuttle had fallen?"

Miss Sleaford turned pale as though living through Saturday's ordeal again.

"No, Mr Nankivell, I can't say I did. No. There was no light. No. It was so dark, we couldn't see a thing properly, and there was such a commotion going on behind us. Had not Mr Hewston suddenly gripped me, I, too, would have fallen down and then...oh, dear..."

She applied herself to her green bottle again and inhaled so deeply that she almost momentarily passed out.

"You have my sympathy, Miss Sleaford. A fearful experience."

"Yes. I still feel very shaky after it, although the exhilaration of yesterday's services did much to cheer my spirit. Poor Mr Harbuttle. Such a dear, worthy man and a good friend of mine."

Evidently the deceased had left one good friend behind him, no matter what others might say. Nankivell felt a wave of sympathetic pity for the little wool shop lady. She had a quiet, old-fashioned dignity about her and standards of conduct to which she rigidly held. This seemed to give her an air of invulnerability, which even Harbuttle must have sensed and respected.

"I think that'll do for the present, Miss Sleaford, and thanks for the help you've given me..." said the officer.

"I'm afraid I haven't helped you at all, Mr Nankivell. I'm a bit confused, and the muddle of things over the weekend seems to have prevented me from thinking properly. I'll get over it in time, I suppose."

"You'll be at the meeting tonight, I take it, Miss Sleaford?"

"Oh, yes. I feel I ought to be there as a senior deacon, although I fear I will not be much help, will I?"

They shook hands. Nankivell threaded his way through the furniture and the shop, with its smell of wool, size, and potpourri. The bell tinkled aggressively, and he found himself once more in the High Street screwing up his eyes at the sudden change of light after the dim interior. He crossed the road and entered the club.

George Mason, the steward of Swarebridge Constitutional Club, was busy polishing glasses in the bar of the billiards room. He had a head of closely cropped hair the shape of a coconut, and he wore a gloomy expression, for his varicose veins had been bothering him again. He greeted Nankivell with a sudden brightening of the countenance. The place was cheerless and deserted, for the habituals had gone home to lunch. There was a strong smell of stale tobacco and beer on the air. The vast expanse of linoleum surrounding and beneath the six large tables was depressing. From a dairy at the back of the club the ceaseless rattle of bottles was nerve-racking.

"Well, George," said the Superintendent. "You've lost a good customer in Alderman Harbuttle, I guess."

"Customer?" croaked the steward, "Customer? The late lamented H'alderman H'aitch never bought a drink for 'imself, 'ard or soft, or for anyone h'else for that matter, durin' the 'ole twenty years I bin 'ere. Nor played snooker. Nor 'ad a game of cards. Nor give a 'alfpenny in tips…"

"Is that so? How did he pass the time?"

"Readin' the papers and argewin'. Reg'lar feller fer argewin' was H'alderman H'aitch. Every day but Sunday for years, except when 'e was on 'olidays at Cleethorpes, — allis went to Cleethorpes did the h'alderman — he'd be at it with anyone as would 'ave a barney with 'im. Throve on it, as you might say."

"Has there been any quarrel or argument you might have overheard lately that could have ended in bad blood, George?"

"Oh, no! Nothin' o' that sort. Mostly political conflict, in a manner o' speakin'. The h'alderman thought a lot of the club members 'ad gone a bit bolshie like and used ter h'air 'is views about the rights of private property and sich. Then a few of his buddies, his cronies like, and him would sit talkin' in front of the newsroom fire, hatchin' things out for the next council meetin'. Wire-pullin', I calls it, between you and me. You'd be surprised, Super, if I was to tell you some of the things I've over'eard in front of that newsroom fire."

"Nothing to cause a murder…?"

George pondered deeply. From the walls photographs of Pogsley, Harbuttle and others, in mayoral regalia, gazed pompously down.

"No, nothin'. But last week — Thursday, I think it was — somethin' 'appened as never did before. Somebody — a chap called Leatherbarrow, who owns a little foundry down Orchard Street — up and tells the h'alderman wat 'e thinks about 'im. Proper scream, it was. The old chap were properly dumbfounded at bein' spoke to so 'eated like. Leatherbarrow, it seems, 'ad some grudge against the corporation about some smell or other risin' from 'is mouldin'-sand dump and the sanitary inspector told 'im, unless 'e shifted it, he'd 'ave him up for committing a nuisance. Well, Mr L runs across 'ere, all 'ot like, to cool 'imself off with a pint, and who does 'e run slap into but H'alderman H'aitch. He tells 'Arbuttle his troubles and the old chap up and defends the sanintary inspector. Tells Mr L the town must be progressive. 'Why, town's motter is "Progress and Plenty," 'e sez, and nearly laughs his own 'ead off at his wit.

"Hup jumps Mr L and tells 'im — all red and squaring-up in his temper — as neether 'im nor any of the rest of the council 'ad an 'alfpennyworth o' progress in any of 'em. 'Look at you,' 'e sez to H'alderman H'aitch, 'are you enny different from wot you was twenty years ago; thirty or forty years ago, come to that? No! You ain't. Same cut o' clothes,' 'e sez, 'same old cock-eyed conservative notions, same old style o' religious teachin' at chapel.' Mr L goes to Zion, too, so 'e's a brother-in-arms, as you might call it, of the h'alderman. 'An' wot's more,' he winds-up, 'wot's more, same ole Duke o' York over the same old routee every year!' That was the last blow, like, a proper narsty one, becos they pulled the h'alderman's leg somethin' shockin' about his foller-me-leader in the dark, and 'e quite liked it. Thought it made 'im into a proper old rip, 'e did…"

Nankivell pricked up his ears. He was just about sick of George and his long, rambling discourse when it struck him that perhaps he might be on to something at last.

"Was the matter pressed further, George?"

"Well, sir, Mr L rushed out at that, but some o' the other chaps starts to twit the h'alderman, who eventually gets in a temper and says he'll show 'em about bein' ole-fashioned and 'idebound. If they want somethin' new for foller-me-leader on Saturday, 'e'll give it 'em. And he starts to mutter to ole Butter-field, oo's been sittin' there quiet-like, drinkin' soda-water on account of havin' water-brash, just like the sceptre at the feast. 'Not through the church,' suddenly 'owls Butterfield. 'I protest.' From which you'd gather that old 'Arbuttle was extendin' the tour of his game and swankin' a bit beforehand. 'Yes and stop me if you can. I'll prove I'm not 'idebound. I'm broad-minded an' a bit of a sport!' With that, I'm called away to serve drinks, see, so I leaves 'em still at it. Made a lot of his foller-me-leader, did Mr H'aitch. His only form of sport, if you asks me, and put his whole 'eart in it."

"Who was in the newsroom when all this was going on, George?"

"When do you mean, sir?"

"When the alderman was quarrelling with Leatherbarrow and then with Butterfield."

George scratched his nut-like head.

"Lemme see …"

The bell from the smoke-room rang suddenly.

"More drinks. Can you just wait a minute till I've done?"

Nankivell looked at his watch. 1.55. He didn't want to keep Hewston waiting.

"Look here, George, think it over and put down a list of all who were in the room on both occasions, when you've a minute to spare, will you?"

"Very good, guvnor…"

The bell rang again, this time more stridently. So, with a good day, George scuttered off.

Nankivell wrote two names in his notebook.

Leatherbarrow. Butterfield.

Then he hurried off to his next appointment.

Mr Hewston was gathering his flock when the Superintendent arrived at the Central School. The boys' playground was, one minute, teeming with a milling, rough, noisy crowd. The next moment, all was still, for Conky had appeared at the door and blown one shrill blast on a whistle. The hush was terrific. One could hear the birds singing and even dead leaves fluttering over the asphalt. Somewhere in the school, a clock struck two. The boys, with hot faces, stood rooted, eager, immobile, like statues, or characters in a scene from the Sleeping Beauty pantomime. Conky blew twice more. The boys began to mark time rhythmically, their feet beating the dust up from the ground. Three blasts, and like a tornado all hurled themselves towards Hewston from every direction and lined up in orderly formation, rank on rank, before him.

From where he stood, Nankivell could see Hewston's mouth opening and closing, fish-like, in some harangue. Five boys detached themselves from the body and sheepishly filed behind the master. The rest, at a word, marched off into school, row by row, followed by a few of the staff who had participated in the parade. With a gesture, Hewston drove the remaining five boys before him and vanished indoors with them.

Nankivell opened the entrance gate, crossed the playground and followed them in.

7

THE WATCHER AT THE CAMP

Nankivell entered the school by the open door. From afar came the chanting of some class or other, already settled down and reciting its lessons in a monotonous singsong. The inspector did not need to travel far beyond the porch, for the first door on the right in the passage was labelled *Headmaster*. It was ajar and Mr Hewston's voice could be heard within, raised in shrill indignation. The sound of it made Nankivell like the fellow less than ever.

"...I smoke, myself. Yes, and I enjoy it. But *I won't have boys of my school surreptitiously puffing in lavatories*, or anywhere else, for that matter. So, I'm going to cane you all. Yes, I shall cane you. And when tempted to smoke again, remember that there's a dose of the same medicine, a larger dose, *much larger*, for you next time. Now...hands first and then, Gubbins...yes, Gubbins, we'll start with you, and *don't snivel*...then you'll each make a back. And one whimper; *and I'll give you some more!!*"

Hewston's voice ranged from a scream when he was threatening his victims to a low purr as he dwelt on the punishment. Like a great cat sadistically playing with a troupe of mice. The man was enjoying it! Nankivell leaned against the wall opposite the open door and waited for the performance to end. The stick could be heard whistling through the air and striking bare flesh and then the muffled seats of trousers. Now and then, there would be a yell from one of the boys or a scuffle as one or another, suffering the agonies of waiting his turn, tried to avoid the rod or put off the evil moment by some subterfuge or other. "Now the other," or "now make a back," and "hold it out or I'll give you some more." Eventually the boys emerged, a motley string of them, red-faced, tight-lipped, blowing on their palms, nursing their hindquarters. Two were struggling to hold back their tears; another was grinning. When they were well out of range of Hewston, Nankivell, whom they had passed silently but in the hope that he'd come to yank Conky off to the lock-up, saw them square their shoulders, make depreciating gestures to each other and then assume a swaggering gait as they disappeared through a door at the end of the corridor to meet and receive the admiration of their fellows and express critical and contemptuous views on Conky's prowess.

The headmaster came to the door of his room, snorting from his efforts, dishevelled but as pleased in appearance as a cat digesting a meal of milk and mice. He started at the sight of his visitor and looked a bit nonplussed. Nankivell had had enough trouble with Conky and his caning in days past. But the man seemed like a drug addict, unable to resist it.

"Ah, Superintendent," panted Hewston. "Unpleasant job just finished… I won't have 'em smoking. I've warned them, but they don't heed. So, they must be punished. I'm a Johnsonian in that respect. The rod isn't used enough these days. If it were, we wouldn't have such unruliness among youngsters."

Nankivell, who himself had smoked in similar places at the age of eleven or thereabouts, made no reply, but uttered a civil greeting.

He followed Hewston into his room and was offered a hard chair from among a plain lot of furniture. The cane lay on a desk. Hewston took it up, bent it fondly in his hands and put it away in a drawer.

"What can I do for you, Superintendent?"

"It's about Saturday evening, Mr Hewston. You, I understand, were next-but-one to Mr Harbuttle when he fell from the gallery."

Hewston nodded assent.

"Did you see a light down below at any time?"

"No, Superintendent, I didn't. Nor did I hear anything. There was such a tumult behind and around me."

"You prevented Miss Sleaford from falling down, too, I hear."

"Yes. I felt her tottering and just managed to pull her clear."

"You've no idea whether or not the file behind you broke before the accident?"

"No. I must confess that I was surprised when he led us into the church. So, it seems was everyone else. But we followed like a flock of sheep. What came over Harbuttle, I don't know…"

"You didn't by any chance see anything unusual on Saturday, Mr Hewston? For example, someone prowling round the kitchens who'd no business there or behaving in a suspicious manner during the game of follow-my-leader. We want to find out who took the knife when the kitchen was empty…say, during the entertainment or when the players were arranging themselves for the game. Nobody seems to have seen intruders in the kitchen, though."

"I'm sure I didn't, Superintendent. Perhaps you might bring something more to light at the meeting this evening, eh?"

"Quite possible. In your capacity as secretary of the church and as one who attends all the meetings there, were you ever struck by enmity between Harbuttle and anyone in particular?"

Hewston's nose dilated as he drew a deep breath.

"Definitely not," he said. "How could such feelings exist between deacons in the same church? There have been bickering, I'll grant you, and resentment at Harbuttle's overbearing ways, but all were soon smoothed over. After all, people got to know the alderman's little foibles and hasty temper. They made allowances."

"In what recent upheavals had he been involved, then?"

Hewston nosed the air contemplatively.

"Well...now this is strictly in private, of course... I don't know that I'm right in mentioning it..."

He smacked his lips. Nankivell knew that he was dying to tell his news, in spite of his simulated reluctance.

"We've been having a bit of trouble with the parson, between you and me. He's married, as you know, but reading between the lines, they're an ill-assorted couple. She's no help to him. Too snobbish, a poor mixer and no tact; says just what she thinks without considering the consequences. A bit of a load on Partington's back, I'm afraid. Recently, he's got a bit too friendly with one of the girls in the choir. There may be nothing in it, of course. Just platonic, you know. Probably. But people are beginning to talk, and when they do in a chapel, it's a very bad thing indeed, as you'll agree. He's been taking her home after choir rehearsals and calling at her people's house on pastoral visits a bit too often. I wouldn't be surprised if that's why Mrs Partington's gone to her mother's, although that's mere guesswork, of course."

Conky's pig-eyes were aglow with enthusiasm for his subject.

"Yes, Mr Hewston, but how does that affect Harbuttle?"

"I'm coming to that, Superintendent. The matter was recently discussed at a private meeting of deacons, without the minister, of course..."

Nankivell could imagine it!

"...and Mr Harbuttle was deputed, in fact, he deputed himself to mention it paternally to Partington. We decided that the parson had just been indiscreet, and a reining-up would do him good. Partington didn't agree. He gave Harbuttle the length of his tongue, told him not to meddle in what didn't concern him and hinted that the alderman's mind wasn't as clean as it might be. He said his own conscience was clear and himself and the lady above reproach. He resented especially the girl's being brought into it. Harbuttle was furious and talked of bringing the whole thing up at a full church meeting next Thursday."

"He did, did he? And what would the result have been?"

"Well... I should say a public scandal. Partington would probably have had to leave the church and would have had a stiff job getting another ministry if he left under a cloud of that kind."

"Did he know that Harbuttle was intending making this public fuss?"

"Yes. The quarrel took place last Wednesday and we heard the result before the deacons' meeting on the following evening. Partington was at the meeting. Made things a bit awkward, of course, but the affair wasn't mentioned in public there. Miss Sleaford told me, however, that the alderman had told the minister what he intended to do. Of course, we knew he'd probably cool off before doing such a thing. Like so many others of Harbuttle's threats, it would just turn out to be a damp squib."

"Who's the girl, by the way, Mr Hewston?"

The headmaster coughed diffidently.

"Well, one hardly likes to drag her in. However... Muriel Arrowsmith. Nice gel. Attractive, but a little flighty. Don't blame the parson, really...hehe! But joking apart, there's no harm in her."

Hewston rung the changes on unctuousness, self-righteousness and man-of-the-worldliness, with a smack of lasciviousness underlying it all.

"I hear that Mr Burt has returned to the fold," said Nankivell by way of changing the subject.

"Yes. A silly quarrel. Tilly never wanted the organ job. Too unladylike for her, I imagine. Rather be among the boys than perched in the organ loft. But Burt insisted. Thank goodness it's settled! Very awkward these squabbles. How is it that some church people are so touchy?"

Nankivell made no answer, although he could have done so in a fashion which would have pained his present companion.

"That's all, then, for the present," said the Superintendent. "I'm grateful for the information and sorry to take up so much of your time. I'll be seeing you at the meeting tonight?"

"Yes. I'll be there."

On the way out, Nankivell put two more names on his list. Partington. Muriel Arrowsmith.

From somewhere in the school a riot seemed to be ensuing. Nankivell could not guess the cause of it, but he knew what would be the result, for his last view of Hewston was of his figure, rushing like a thunderbolt through the door at the end of the corridor.

* * *

Mr Henry Roebuck, of Moore, Roebuck, Cadby-Tripp & Roebuck, was Clerk to the Justices of Swarebridge and in that capacity had become a close friend and admirer of Nankivell. During the sittings of the local Court of Petty Sessions, at which the Superintendent was a regular party for the prosecution, the forensic blundering and fumbling of the bench caused Mr Roebuck no end of trouble. At such times, he had only to look in the direction of Nankivell's seat, which resembled a churchwarden's pew, to receive a twinkling, sympathetic glance. It ended by the pair of them having a secret understanding, almost a private joke against the magistrates. The lawyer, therefore, received his visitor cordially.

Roebuck was seated at a large untidy desk in one of a suite of six rooms which his firm occupied over the Bank of Brentshire. In the five other rooms were the general staff, and Messrs

Moore, Cadby-Tripp, Roebuck (Harold) respectively, and a number of clients waiting to receive advice. Roebuck (Henry) was small, middle-aged, thin and extremely active. He had a face like Mr Punch, except perhaps not so fantastic about the nose, chin and crown of the head. The latter has a tonsure surrounded by a fairly thick, dark thatch, just as if its owner had decided to become a monk and then abandoned the project in the chair of the monastic barber. He was signing letters when the Superintendent entered his private office. Furiously and illegibly he drove his pen across the face of each sheet after meticulously scrutinising its six-and-eight-pence-worth of advice.

"Right!" said Mr Roebuck, flinging the mass of correspondence into a wire basket marked "Post" and with a gesture of finality against which no appeal to a higher court was permissible. "Hullo, Nankivell, I'm ready for you." He did not produce Harbuttle's will but seemed to have very thoroughly digested it.

"Quite a simple affair," he said after preliminary small talk and a short preamble to the effect that the deceased had left behind him no blood relatives other than his daughter and her offspring. "Here it is. Don't bother to take it down. I'll see you get a *précis* of it. Probable total of estate after death duties and bank trustee fees, and legacies to the bank manager and me of fifty pounds apiece, is £15,000. He'd already made over his business to his daughter, so there'll be no death duties on that. Estate divided as follows: one, a thousand pounds to Zion Chapel. Two, another thousand pounds to the Swarebridge Boys' Grammar School to institute an open university scholarship named the "Samuel Harbuttle Exhibition" (exhibition!!). Three, one thousand pounds to Miss Sleaford. Not so strange as it seems, although it isn't generally known that she lent him five hundred pounds of her small capital, which he paid back later, when he almost went bust in his business years ago when Swarebridge was just a village. I prepared the papers, so I know.

After he recovered himself, thanks to the loan, he never forgot Miss Sleaford. You see, she trusted him when the bank and his so-called pals turned him down. Next, an annuity of two pounds a week for Mrs Merchant, his housekeeper. Cost about £1,500. A hundred for his kitchen maid and two hundred and fifty for his gardener. Residue of about £10,000 as follows: Three thousand to his daughter outright. Rest in trust for grandchildren with income to mother for life. That just stops Singleton, who's a bit of a fool, using it all up by losing it in the shop, which he's not handling at all well. That's the lot."

"Seems a very fair sort of will to me," said Nankivell.

"I agree. Carefully thought out and fundamentally sound. In cold blood, the old chap wasn't a bad sort; he was at his worst in company!"

"So," continued the little lawyer, "If you want motives you've got a weary lot of possibilities." He raised a podgy, well-kept hand and ticked off his fingers.

"Suspect A. Treasurer of Zion, old Butterfield, who wants a legacy to balance his accounts. Ridiculous, because they're rolling in money left by Pogsley.

"B. Grammar School youth, eager to get cash to go to university. Also absurd, as Euclid impolitely remarks.

"C. Mrs Merchant and Miss Sleaford, jointly or severally. No good, as neither nor both are capable of despatching anybody with a knife.

"D. The Singletons. Ah! Not likely to be her; but he might have got sick of waiting. Try Singleton…"

"Thanks for the analysis," smiled Nankivell. "I'll bear it well in mind and when I haul Singleton up before the bench, please see that they don't sentence him to death on the spot, which they'll probably do, if I know 'em. I'm grateful for the information, too. And now can you spare the time for a trip to Pisgah?"

"That's exactly what I *am* ready for," said the lawyer and after drinking enjoyably from a bottle containing very yellow-looking water and changing his spectacles, he took up his hat and gloves, seized Nankivell affectionately by the arm and steered him to his waiting car.

The visit to Pisgah yielded nothing whatever. Together the two men went through private papers but found nothing to help in the case. Bills, political pamphlets, speeches, sermons in the dead man's sprawling hand abounded. At five o'clock, they admitted they'd drawn a blank and prepared to depart.

"Sorry you've had a fruitless trip, Superintendent," said Roebuck, bundling together a number of unpaid bills, a pass-book and some unused cheques. "There'll be nothing in his box at the bank, either, except deeds of property, investments and the like. He and I went through it last week. He seems to have destroyed most of his correspondence, except business stuff and a bundle of his late wife's early and intimate letters to him, which we must burn, too."

"Yes. It's obvious we'll have to try some other trail. A pity, Mr Roebuck, but there it is," retorted Nankivell and sauntered to the window, lighting a cigarette on the way. The room was stuffy, and the Superintendent opened the French window which overlooked a vast expanse of countryside. There was a small balcony outside made in the form of a sun lounge, with an iron chair on it. Probably Harbuttle's look-out as he viewed the landscape o'er. Nankivell took up the field-glasses, which still remained where he had left them earlier in the day, and half absently swung them here and there, picking out objects in the distance.

Slowly he moved them in a horizontal arc and brought them to rest first on one landmark, then on another. The distant camp on Whitestone Ring was agog with the searchlight unit. Nankivell made out plainly the uniformed figures of men he'd seen about the town when they were off duty. At the entrance to the camp stood a sentry-box and the Superintendent was rather surprised to see, standing before it, a stocky figure in full kit and with a rifle and fixed bayonet, employed in a similar occupation to his own. The soldier was sweeping his field of vision with a powerful pair of service binoculars, probably issued for plane-spotting when needed and now serving to pass the time. Gradually the glasses of the uniformed watcher described a course approaching Pisgah and then stopped. The Superintendent and the soldier were examining each other over the long distance! Nankivell experienced a queer sensation of conquering great space as if by magic.

The uniformed man raised his free hand in a jocular salute. Nankivell followed suit. Then, the sentry made a series of gestures indicating boredom, heat, hunger, thirst and finally vulgar disgust at his occupation.

"Whatever are *you* doing there?" asked the lawyer, who had now finished his task and was watching his companion capering on the veranda.

"Just making the acquaintance of one of the boys at the camp. He's a sentry and was watching this place..."

"Humph. You were cutting some queer antics between you!"

Nankivell coloured under his tan.

"You know, Mr Roebuck," he said thoughtfully, "That fellow might have seen things happening here that would interest me. I'll go to the camp as soon as I've time and have a chat with them."

Suddenly, Nankivell felt weary. There seemed so much to do and yet he'd hardly stopped all day. And there was that confounded church assembly later in the evening. He was glad Roebuck had brought his car and he decided to leave the camp and its occupants until tomorrow after the inquest.

On the way out the two men passed Mrs Merchant. She was all smiles. Roebuck had told her, in confidence, the news that she had been remembered in the will and the extent of her benefit, and her cup of joy was full.

8

SCANDALOUS AFFAIR AT THE
CHURCH MEETING

When Nankivell arrived at the Sunday school, the place was already humming with an assorted crowd of genuine or curious people, hobnobbing away and very jocular about it all. The solemnity of the occasion and the cloud generated by the previous Saturday's tragedy had been dispelled and the gathering was taking the form of a pleasant social function. Volumes of steam and the gurgling of gas-geysers in the kitchen announced that tea was being made, and Nankivell would not have been greatly surprised if someone had suggested a glee by the choir or a song by one of the many soloists present.

On the arrival of the police, Mr Partington appointed himself informal chairman and, endeavouring to restore order out of chaos, bade all be seated. The Superintendent, who disliked the whole business, joined the minister on the platform, and the shepherd of the flock then asked him to make known his wishes to the sheep. The latter were now arranged on long benches set in rows in the body of the hall. A number of women had brought children, who misjudging the occasion for an outing, clamoured noisily and ran about the room with shrill cries. These having been more or less subdued, one woman was heard excusing herself loudly for bringing her son, a small, mischievous, peevish-looking boy of about eight, dressed in a sailor suit, which he had outgrown. He was holding a whistle, fastened round his neck by a lanyard, and from time to time blew a blast on it. Whereupon, his mother tore the instrument from his mouth with a fury suggesting that she wished to extract whistle and all his teeth as well in one sweep and shook him violently until he fell into a form of stupor.

"Willie's father's doing ARP tonight and I couldn't leave 'im," she apologised.

"Want a drink of water," wailed Willie, surnamed Pole, and was again furiously shaken into a coma.

The deacons ranged themselves on the front row; at the back were the members of the Young Ladies' Class; and still more to the rear, the Young Men's Class, greatly attenuated through loss of strength to the Forces. Light dalliance, tittering and whispered but insincere protests were bandied about in this part of the hall from time to time. A young man in RAF uniform was beside himself with joy to find on his first leave, that Tilly Burt was again in the fold, and he took the opportunity to ask her if he might see her home, to which she consented, blushing and bright-eyed. Her father had been received back like a lost sheep by his fellow deacons, who, feeling that he had returned to support them in their darkest hour, pressed his hand fervently and, although not yet officially re-elected to their body, he was perched among them with Charlie Singleton on one side and Butterfield on the other.

The latter looked more dyspeptic than ever after the week-end's ordeal, whilst Charlie, joint principal mourner, through marriage, of Mr Harbuttle, was dressed in black, his round, insipid, pale face set in lines becoming his bereavement and his thin, fair hair plastered across his head as though he had copiously anointed it with his own butter for the occasion. His wife had stayed at home, thinking it meet that one so smitten should keep house for the time being. Behind these three pillars of Zion sat Willie and his mother, the former blowing gently down his whistle and generally disturbing the peace. Now and then, one of the trio turned and eye-browed or glared at the boy, but without success, although some of the efforts of Mr Butterfield would have turned a normal child into a pillar of salt.

"...We are very anxious to find out if anyone saw an intruder in the kitchen at any time, especially handling knives..."

Someone stifled a scream and a woman addicted to fainting on the slightest provocation was hustled into the fresh air of the school yard.

"Mother, mother," said Willie Pole, "I was playing on the stairs and I saw..."

Mrs Pole, intent on what the policeman was saying, shook her offspring more vigorously than ever by the arm until his teeth rattled and his sailor cap, which he insisted on keeping on his head in spite of all efforts, slid over his face and almost smothered him.

"... Then some of you may possibly have seen intruders or others behaving suspiciously. We want details of that, too. Anything, no matter how trivial, should be reported. For example, did anyone see Alderman Harbuttle involved in any squabbles recently? We also want to know what he did from arriving here to join the afternoon procession up to the time of his death..."

From the ranks of young ladies rose a wild sobbing, as one of them broke down under the strain. Her friend assisted her from the room, and together they ran the gauntlet of hundreds of eyes to the door.

"... No. Please don't all speak at once. Sergeant Cresswell is in one of the classrooms and will take your brief statements. If you have information of any importance, we'll make a personal call on you later. Please be as brief as possible and only give information if it really concerns the case. Thank you."

Relieved to be through the harangue, Nankivell stepped from the stage and approached various persons he had seen in the gathering, with a view to arranging for fuller interviews in private later. Butterfield, Singleton, Partington, Hewston, Leatherbarrow, all were there.

Tea appeared. One after another slipped portentously into the classroom where the unseen Cresswell was waiting for them. Cups and saucers rattled; gossip flowed freely. Darkness had fallen and the caretaker had drawn the black-out curtains and switched on the lights. The night was fine and clear and a number of mixed couples slipped away from the back rows of seats, glad to take advantage of the occasion for a bit of extra pleasure in each other's company.

"Mother, mother," persisted Willie Pole, "I want to tell you something..."

Mrs Pole pushed a scalding cup of tea in the boy's hand and did not stop her spate of chatter to the group of matrons who stood around her, smacking their lips, nodding and clicking their teeth with dismay at some scandalous incident which Air-Raid-Warden Pole had patrolled into. Willie still tugged at her coat.

"Now look here," hissed the exasperated mother, "I'll give you a good smackin' if you don't behave. Look, there's Edgar Mason, on his own. Go and play with him, like a good boy, but don't go far away." Willie, gingerly carrying his cup, approached his smaller friend. Edgar was chubby and red-cheeked and was also struggling with a cup of boiling tea whilst his mother, one of the Marthas of Zion, brewed more among the geysers. After the usual formalities, friendly relations were established between the two and Willie led off Edgar to a deserted class-room, where he initiated him into the mysteries of drinking tea out of a saucer.

Under the stimulus of tea, the hearts of all in the gathering warmed towards the police. Nankivell's demeanour and efficient bearing had won their confidence and they were almost joyful in their assurance that before long, the malefactor would be brought to justice. The passage of time had already begun to put matters in their proper perspective and those who spent sleepless hours after Saturday's terrible happenings fancying the end of everything had come, now began to find the sharp edge going from their imaginings and other interests violently obtruding. After all, in war-time, with joining the forces, coming home on leave, embarking for unknown parts, rationing and billeting, and the care and discipline of evacuees, one's thoughts soon turn from murder, even if a Harbuttle *is* involved and that on one's own doorstep, or, as Mr Maw, a deacon, put it, "on the steps of the h'altar of the thrice happy place our souls delight in."

So, we see the people of Zion gathered together again in calmer mood, in friendly intercourse. The tea flows freely, there is talk of the round of social functions involved in the winter programme of the church and some, before poor Harbuttle is below ground, find a blessing in his departure, for he was the last of a long line of stalwarts opposed to the playing of whist in the school and furthermore, during his presence at gatherings, no one dared to suggest the most sedate form of dancing. These restrictions now removed, a party of women is already informally arranging a whist-drive and dance for a Saturday not far ahead. Mr Partington looks around, notes the atmosphere of calm after the storm, seeks in vain for the very attractive form of Miss Arrowsmith, and then is suddenly surrounded by a body of matrons, who, with the twin ideas of protecting him from scandalous dalliance with Muriel and obtaining his agreement to card-playing in the precincts, erect a protective fence around him with their spreading forms. They are making fine progress in obtaining the parson's concurrence in their revolutionary schemes when, of a sudden, in the midst of this bliss, from a classroom at the back of the hall a wild, hysterical, feminine voice rings out:

"Take that! And that! You common Irish trollop!!"

This startling interruption is punctuated by two resounding smacks.

* * *

THE CRIES and tears heard earlier in the meeting from among the young ladies were those of Muriel Arrowsmith and the friend who led her out to stifle them was Mary O'Dare, a young typist of Pogsley's Mills. Mary was an Irish girl who had, about two years earlier, arrived to earn her own living in Swarebridge. She was a distant cousin of Mr Tinker, assistant-secretary of the Sunday School, lodged at his home, and attended Zion on his persuasion. She was a small, trim, dark-haired, blue-eyed girl, who, thanks to her pleasant ways and ready wit, soon became very popular at the church. At the time of the turmoil in Zion, she had several young men competing for her favours and was making up her mind which to choose. Muriel Arrowsmith had become one of her friends, though not the closest of them.

Now Muriel was a very attractive girl and to understand why she was thirty-one and unmarried requires some research into family history. Her father, Richard Arrowsmith, was a nondescript little chap and foreman in Pogsley's warehouse. He had no claim whatever to distinction in Zion, a little, thin, knock-kneed man, he was a mere private soldier in the ranks of the churchgoers; a complete nonentity. But his wife was different. A dumpy, apple-cheeked woman from distant parts and a thoroughgoing snob. How she came to marry a decent nobody like Richard, no one ever knew, except that perhaps he had caught her on the rebound from some more suitable but less decided suitor. Mrs Arrowsmith's father never failed during his lifetime to bewail his lot of a stonemason, which, he bitterly asserted, was due to a remote ancestor being cheated out of vast lands and monies which were his birth right, by an unscrupulous relative. Mrs Arrowsmith had been a Molineux, pronounced in French fashion by her daughter, Mollinew by her one-time neighbours in distant parts, and Mullinaxe by those who spoke it in Swarebridge. She brought her daughter up, thanks to her disappointment in the social and monetary progress of her husband, to believe that she was blue-blooded and entitled to carry armorial bearings, and this failing made itself manifest in Muriel's dealings with the opposite sex. The lowly dared not approach her amorously; the higher born wouldn't. Thus we find this Juno of a girl, tall, well-built, dark of hair and eyes, with a lovely Greek profile, ripe lips and gleaming teeth, whose graces should have been making one man, at least, delirious with joy, still on the shelf at past thirty.

On leaving the main hall the two girls took to the open air until Muriel had recovered her composure and then, the night being a bit chilly, they retired to a small, empty classroom indoors. There Mary O'Dare, unable to understand the sudden display of grief, invited her friend's confidence. It was then that Muriel disclosed the startling news that during the entertainment on the previous Saturday, Mr Harbuttle had whispered to her that he would like a word with her on private business in one of the classrooms. Thinking it was something concerning the forthcoming games, she had followed him under cover of the darkness due to the performance of a dialogue on the stage. To her surprise, the alderman had proposed to her, offered to make her a lady, endow her with all his worldly wealth, install her in Pisgah without any duties to soil her hands, and had urged her to make him the happiest man in Swarebridge at once.

Muriel knew how greatly the parson admired her and she, in turn, was just on the verge of falling in love with him. Nevertheless, she encouraged him only in what she thought was a discreet fashion, which the rest of the women of Zion thought highly disgusting. Mr Partington, however, had a wife and no money or ancestry worth thinking of, so, of late, bitterness had entered Muriel's heart. Instead of asking her to fly with him and be damned to the consequences, Mr P had simply manifest great excitement in her presence, sedately taken her home after certain choir rehearsals, and called frequently on her parents and talked most of the time with her father. Wealth, rank, a house like a castle, servants to wait upon her, an old man's devotion, Harbuttle could offer all these. Only the Adonis of her dreams and the "Mr Right" of her mother's were missing. She had smiled on the alderman after recovering from the first assault, told him that she liked him very, very much, and left him almost certain of an affirmative after duly thinking it over at weekend.

Then, Harbuttle had died with a knife in his chest. Terrified, Muriel had mentioned the proposal to no one, thinking that Partington himself, having overheard the interview — for she was sure she'd heard the creak of boots outside the classroom — had smitten his successful rival dead. In a burst of emotional weakness, she opened her heart to her Irish friend.

Judge of Muriel's astonishment when Mary burst into peals of merry laughter.

"Don't worry," said the colleen. "Mr Partington was far enough away. And as for the end of your romance, there's as good, far better, fish in the sea… Harbuttle proposed to me a fortnight ago and I turned him down!"

Muriel reacted strangely. Instead of finding consolation in the alderman's peddling himself in the marriage market, she was seized by violent rage at being his second string. All the thwarted, pent-up emotions of years and the tremendous anxiety of the weekend burst forth in a torrent of anger.

"You little liar!" she screamed. "You're making fun of me."

Mary's Irish blood rose at once.

"Nobody calls an O'Dare a liar... Take it back..." she retorted, her eyes blazing.

"Never!" replied the infuriated Juno. "And take that and that, you common Irish trollop!"

* * *

THESE AWFUL WORDS uttered by an angry, unseen speaker echoed across the room, struck everybody dumb with amazement and brought an anxious momentary hush to the gathering. Then, Mrs Arrowsmith rose from the body of the hall and strode purposively to the classroom, followed by a motley crowd, headed by Mrs Tinker, the protectress of Mary O'Dare.

"Shut your mouth and leave me alone..." is heard from the unseen disputants and then bedlam breaks out. Mrs Arrowsmith in restrained fashion endeavours to separate the combatants, who are now holding each other by the arms as if about to execute a complicated tango step, but in her pacific efforts, becomes involved in the dance. Her temper roused, she boxes Mary on the ears. Mrs Tinker entering the room witnesses this outrage and wades in.

There is naturally much inter-marriage among Zionists, and in times of trouble families are united, those with even the most attenuated blood connections arraying themselves with their kith and kin. The dispute over Harbuttle and his offers of marriage, therefore, grows into a miniature war of the roses. In no time, the classroom is filled to overflowing with a crowd of angry, milling women, pushing each other about, afraid to smite hard but resorting to jostling, charging, thrusting and pulling tactics and using arms, elbows, bosoms, hindquarters and knees like battering rams. The noise is appalling. Speech flows freely and angry, vulgar words rush forth in torrents. Place, dignity, decorum are all forgotten in this release of pent-up feelings. The saintly, peace-loving women who one by one thrust themselves in the doorway of the room hoping in some way to calm the storm, are unwillingly sucked into the maelstrom and, before they know where they are, are rampaging with the rest. The men, dumbfounded and nonplussed, hang back, knowing that once they intrude, the bloody masculine forms of combat may supervene and replace the more dishevelled and shrill, but less deadly feminine type. Nankivell, who has been assisting Cresswell in his temporary office, arrives astonished on the scene and is relieved to find that Mrs Nankivell is outside the sphere of action, but looking helplessly round for some way of ending the hostilities. The racket of the battlefield is deafening and faintly resembles the unanimous barracking of a referee at a football match or the bidding at a gargantuan auction sale many times magnified. Suddenly, relief arrives in the shape of Mrs Butterfield.

This good woman, huge in bulk, slow of movement and not easily disturbed, decides that it is time she took a hand. She rises from the seat on which she has been sitting somewhat complacently listening to the tumult, waddles across the main hall and with difficulty squeezes herself through the door of the classroom. Like a battleship, she steers her course to the very heart of the fray, elbowing protagonists apart until she reaches the vortex. Muriel Arrowsmith and Mary O'Dare stand helpless and appalled at the furious typhoon of wrath they have released. The sight of Mrs Butterfield's massive figure in their midst strikes the warring parties with terror and they drag themselves apart, peacemakers and combatants each hoping to goodness that she isn't going to throw her weight in with the opposing side.

"That'll do," laconically wheezes Mrs Butterfield, standing arms akimbo. "I'm ashamed of the lot of you. What do you think you're doing in this holy place? Do you want to cause a split in the church and disgrace us all before the Episcopalians and ranters? Just stop it at once and make friends again!"

She looms there, a tower of menacing pacifism not to be

gainsaid, and her awful forecast of a schism in the chapel petrifies them. To this is added the fact that Mr Butterfield shortly hopes to become a director of Pogsleys (1927) Ltd, on whom their daily bread depends. Soon, a few peaceable ones are seen smiling sheepishly at each other; others weep with shame. The lion lies down with the lamb; previous antagonists assist in straightening each other's clothing and hair. One by one the hot, dishevelled women, driven forth by Mrs Butterfield, return to the men, who, relieved at not seeing them carried out half-killed, smile and greet them, ready to say no more about it. In their relief, some of the males whose wives are reputed to wear the trousers in their households, rush to the geysers intent on making more tea. One or two stragglers recovering from hysterics and a few intransigents swearing to meet and renew the fray as soon as possible, remain behind. Muriel and Mary are persuaded to kiss each other and become reconciled, ostensibly if not in fact. Peace is gradually restored and is expressed in a species of holy glee, giving rise to beaming faces, chuckling speech and such palavering and pollydoodling as never was. But the new calm is shattered.

A shrill scream is heard in the quiet room to which, earlier in the evening, Willie Pole had retired to drink tea from a saucer. His mother has been hunting for him after the fray and now reels to the door, wails and falls unconscious over the threshold. Nankivell, standing bewildered after this phantasmagoria of emotion, is first at Mrs Pole's side and, leaving her to those who follow him, enters the classroom. He soon emerges, his face pale and grim, closes the door and asks someone to fetch a doctor.

Willie Pole, his head muffled in a large overcoat and with someone's scarf tied cruelly round his neck, is lying dead on the floor beside a half-empty cup of tea!

9

THE SHEEP AND THE GOATS

From the foregoing description it might be assumed that the good people of Zion were callous and tended lightly to regard the death of Samuel Harbuttle. Nothing is farther from the truth, however. At the first sign of disaster they closed their ranks, which were only temporarily and superficially riven by two silly spinsters. Unable to open the safety valves of emotion by swearing, drinking, or beating-up their connubial partners, they had to keep each other in good heart and of a cheerful countenance by social intercourse. The hubbub at the Monday evening meeting before the second murder, then, did not arise out of levity; the excited conversation was aimed at maintaining morale. Even the tea so vigorously brewed was to keep up spirits under great stress.

The death of Willie Pole, however, caused a change in the temper of the church. Three score years and ten, violently cut off at the end of its span, is bad enough; but a child murdered at its play is another matter! Immediate justice was demanded. Instead of exhibiting terror, the people of Zion were seized by an urgent zeal, a holy fervour to stamp out the monster in their midst. They ranged themselves behind the police solidly. Harbuttle might have been killed by some stray outsider, but Willie could only have met his death at the hands of a member of the community of Zion. The church could not rest nor even function until the rotten limb had been removed and cast into the burning.

It was midnight before Nankivell persuaded the last of the stupefied assembly to go home and then he joined Patchett at the police station. There, with Cresswell in the offing, they held a conference.

"This is about the worst thing I've ever come across," Nankivell told his subordinate. "As might be expected, young Pole's mother was frantic. You see, she blamed herself for sending him to play and not heeding him much. But the bitterest pill of all for her seems to be that the lad wanted to tell her something and she wouldn't listen to him. Preferred gossiping instead."

"Any idea what it was?" interjected Patchett.

"As far as I could gather between the poor woman's cries, young Willie was trying to tell her he saw someone. That was after my query about seeing anybody playing with the knives in the deserted kitchen. Mrs Pole shook him and told him to be quiet, little thinking that he might have seen the murderer choosing his weapon."

"My God! And the murderer must have overheard it and taken advantage of the commotion in the classroom to shut the poor kid's mouth for good."

"That's it, Patchett. On Saturday, it appears, young Pole and another lad, Edgar Mason, who was there tonight and whom I had a word with, went off to play during a bit of a sketch the young men were giving. The youngsters had been restless, and their parents thought they'd let them run off a bit of energy before going home, so let 'em off to enjoy themselves. They started playing hide-and-seek. When it was Willie's turn to hide, it seems he tried the kitchen, which he thought was empty, and came rushing out, saying that there was somebody there. That must have been Harbuttle's murderer. Little Mason says Willie Pole seemed a bit scared, but didn't say who it was, and shortly after that, their parents came for them to go home."

"Yes?"

"Willie must have remembered this when I asked if anyone had seen intruders in the kitchen, and started to tell his mother, who silenced him. She said he was shouting excitedly at her. Anyone around could hear. Now, even if Willie *didn't* see the murderer — let's assume it might have just been one of the helpers tidying-up he saw — probably the killer heard footsteps whilst he was taking the knife. He can't risk young Pole talking. He must shut him up some way. He sees the two boys go into the classroom with their tea. Then, young Mason tells me, he left Willie because he'd drunk all his own tea and wanted some more. The murderer guesses little Pole is alone and seeks some excuse to get at him. He must find out whether he's been seen by the boy. Then, as if by magic, that silly quarrelling breaks out in a nearby classroom and under cover of it, whoever did the foul trick gets Willie alone, perhaps questions him and finds him terrified and beginning to scream, so stifles him and kills him."

"And didn't anyone see anybody entering the room where the boy's body was found, Super?"

"Not a soul. He must have chosen his time, and everyone was intent on making peace elsewhere. As for who might have over-heard Willie arguing with his mother. Well, there were forty or more people round, I reckon. A row of deacons in front, ranks of women on each side and another row of men behind. It's got me stumped."

"What's the next move then, Chief?"

"Let's sort out the information we've got at present. Here,

Cresswell, draw up a chair to the desk and let's make out some kind of an orderly account of the bits and pieces of information you gathered tonight and last Saturday."

The three men drew together and Nankivell took a writing pad and pencil. Notebooks were compared and sifted and after a full hour's work a summary of their investigations to date took shape. Patchett had done little research in the matter at all. Other duties and inquest formalities had kept him occupied, so Nankivell, as much to get the case clear in his own mind as to keep his subordinate informed, went through their findings item by item.

"So far as we've gone," said the Superintendent, "Let's look at those who might wish to see the end of Harbuttle. Quite a lot of people hated him and would have liked to see the last of him but wouldn't have gone as far as killing him. Now, who, in particular would benefit by his death?"

Nankivell ticked off his points on his fingers.

"First, there's his family, Singleton. Next, Butterfield. We might also include the parson, Partington, and Hewston, the schoolmaster."

"They seem a strange lot, to be sure," said Patchett stroking his chin. "Especially the parson."

"Yes. I'd better run through the reasons for including them. Singleton, to begin with, is an obvious suspect. The shop isn't doing well. Singleton is an unenterprising sort of chap and has lost ground to the multiple stores, especially since rationing began in earnest. That's common property and, no doubt, he's feeling the pinch. Under Harbuttle's energetic management the place managed to pay, but we mustn't forget that the alderman's fortune was made mainly from land speculation and not in groceries. There's too much competition in Swarebridge."

"Still," interposed Patchett, "that's not enough to make a man commit murder, is it?"

"No. But we must add to it the fact that Harbuttle and his

son-in-law didn't hit it off together. Remember, his daughter married against his wishes and he never forgave Singleton for getting the better of him there. They've had words, the three of them, on the way the business was declining and Harbuttle has made a public show a time or two, of his contempt for Singleton."

"All the same, Singleton's a milk-and-water sort of fellow. Not a murderer at all. Had he any alibi, Chief?"

"No. He and his wife left during the entertainment to take the children off to bed. He told me he went right home and stayed in afterwards. Nobody can check that but his wife, so we don't get much forrader there. But here's something. When Singleton was gathering his hat and coat from the hooks in the passage at the back of the school — you know the corridor from which some of the classrooms are entered? — he overheard Harbuttle proposing to Muriel. So did the parson. Partington told me after the unholy row which occurred between the two women and seemed to involve most of the other ladies in the end. Partington was getting his hat and coat, too, and came upon Singleton unawares."

"Ah. Now that's a more likely motive, eh?"

"Yes, because what's going to happen if the old man weds again? He'll make another will, leaving the bulk to his new wife. Can you conceive Singleton getting so mad that he went out for the old man's blood right away?"

"Oh, I daresay he might. But what about Mrs Singleton? Is she going to shield him with an alibi — not much use, I'll grant — when her own father is the victim?"

"She was never fond of her father, remember, for what he'd done to her and her husband and the way he treated her mother when she was alive."

"Yes, Chief, but blood's thicker than water..."

"She's stuck to Singleton in spite of everything and might be prepared to go farther still. All the same, let it pass for the time being. By the same token, the parson might have got mad. He's sweet on Muriel, too, and furthermore, Harbuttle has tried to make a scandal about it, threatened to get the fellow sacked if he didn't behave himself. We can understand why, if the old chap was sweet on Muriel himself."

"Still…a parson. It sounds rather a tall order, eh?"

"Yes. But put him among the faintly possible. I'll call on Partington tomorrow and hear what he has to say for himself."

"What about Butterfield? *Some* murderer, if you ask me."

"He's a motive, too, but whether or not he'd rise to killing is another matter. I mention him, however, as a potential enemy of Harbuttle and a powerful one, too. For years, Butterfield's been waiting for a seat on the board of Pogsley's. He's been with them since he was a lad, he's a high officer and, from what I gather, the directors have great confidence in him. So much so, that at the next general meeting his name goes forward for the seat on the board made vacant by the death of Claude Frost. Now, here's the rub. Harbuttle's a big shareholder, too. More so than Butterfield, although the latter has the better moral claim, shall we say. Of late, Harbuttle's decided he'd like a place among Pogsley's directors and has been canvassing his shareholder pals. It was touch and go which of 'em got the vacant job. Perhaps Butterfield, at the sight of his life's ambition being snatched from under his very nose by one of Harbuttle's calibre, got tough. It's worth considering, however."

"But he had an alibi. He was in the queue behind the alderman when the old chap was killed, and several people said they heard him arguing and protesting when the alderman led them into church."

"Just so. All the same, we mustn't forget it was dark and someone cunning enough might have slipped the file and nipped down to where the alderman fell. Rather a long shot, but not to be overlooked."

"Hm. Very unlikely, Chief, if I may say so."

"Partington had an alibi, too, if we believe his tale. He was on the way to the station to meet the minister for the morrow. His companion wasn't there tonight, so I've that to check."

"Did you say Hewston, too?"

"I just mentioned him as an enemy. How he could have broken file, I can't see, for he rescued Miss Sleaford from falling down the trap as well. Hewston's the butt of Harbuttle's extreme spite. As church secretary, he's bullied at meetings and humiliated before the rest of the deacons. He daren't say much or resign, because he holds a job under the education committee and Harbuttle was deputy chairman at the time of his death. Then again, as you know very well, Hewston's been before the committee for caning kids. Some of the parents have been to see us here about taking it to court and we've managed to pacify them by saying we'd warn Hewston. Lucky for him we've plenty of influence in the town. Can you conceive a man of Hewston's temperament, bullyragged at every turn, unhealthy and introspective, knuckling under to his superiors and venting his spleen on his pupils, can you conceive him developing a kind of obsession, a persecution mania with Harbuttle as its focus and finally working out a clever way of disposing of the old man. Could he possibly have stabbed Harbuttle *before* he fell?"

"We're theorising very much, aren't we, chief?"

"Yes, I want to turn this over fully in my mind and I'm airing improbabilities as well as possibilities. You're very quiet, Cresswell. Haven't you any ideas?"

The sergeant turned a deep red. To tell the truth, he was almost asleep. He had been up late on duty the previous two nights and a further spell in the small hours was one too many for him.

"I've been listening, sir," he said. "Takin' all in, so to speak, and then, by your leave, I'll think it over a bit after a night's sleep."

"Well, there's one other point, and then we'll call it a day..."

Patchett's eyes twinkled and he seemed to struggle to refrain from commenting on the fact that it was past two of a new day already.

"... This morning I had a word with George, the steward at the club, about what someone said was a bet made by Harbuttle to take his procession through the church itself on Saturday night. It turned out hardly to be a bet but amounted to a rather impulsive retort to a taunt made by Leatherbarrow, the little man with the foundry, you know, that he was out-of-date in everything he did. George left Harbuttle and Butterfield arguing about the propriety of daring to play follow-my-leader in church."

Patchett guffawed loudly.

"That's not true to type in Harbuttle," he said. "Why, he was a perfect stickler for what he called the decencies of religious bodies. He opposed dancing and card-playing in the school. He must have gone barmy doing what he did..."

"Yes. His thoughts were turning to marrying a girl a lot younger than himself. I guess he thought he'd have to show himself broad-minded. A queer way of doing it, but there it was. Now, someone must have known that he was going through the church and must have opened the trapdoor and lain doggo, waiting for him to fall through. I thought after talking to George, that the fact that Harbuttle proposed a new route was hardly likely to become the talk of the town, although to some of these little provincials it might mean almost the end of the world. However, I asked for a list of all those who were within earshot when this talk about traipsing through the chapel was in full swing. He gave it to me as I passed tonight."

Nankivell took a grubby slip of paper and with difficulty deciphered the handwriting of the steward.

"Mr Alderman Harbuttle," he read. "Messrs Butterfield,

Leatherbarrow (left in middle of talk), Aspden, Burt, Singleton, Fish and Swarbrick."

"A mixed lot," said Patchett. "Butterfield and Singleton are on your list already. Leatherbarrow, Fish and Swarbrick were as likely as not at the club when the old man was killed. They haunt the place and could be checked-up. What about Burt?"

"Oh, Burt had just made it up with Zion folk. You remember his quarrel about his daughter's not getting the organist's job and how he took himself and his family off. It seems he's friends again and to show it, went and cut up the ham and tongue for the party. He claims to be an expert in that line. Harbuttle was a ringleader in getting the girl turned down, although, judging from accounts of her playing, nobody blamed him. I gather that Burt was on speaking terms with the alderman again on Saturday."

"What about his alibi?"

"I had a word with him tonight. He says at the time the crime was committed, he was down at Moggridge's Farm at Leather Lea, two miles away, and that Moggridge will confirm. So that's a job for you, tomorrow, Patchett."

Patchett smiled and couldn't resist a last dig.

"Thought you were going to say go and get the old chap out of bed now and check-up, Chief. An eccentric old codger, and no mistake, is Moggy..."

Cresswell finally succumbed and emitted a sort of apologetic snore. Nankivell looked at him and smiled. The sergeant's jaw had dropped, and his pleasant, round face had grown elongated and weary looking from exhaustion.

"Unkind of me to keep you chaps here until this time," said Nankivell. "I must be a bit excited about this crime wave and I'm forgetting myself. Let's be getting along. I'll drive the pair of you home. *Cresswell!!*"

The police sergeant leapt to his feet and made sparring

gestures. Then realising what he had done, he looked despairingly around.

"Don't bother to excuse yourself, Cresswell. Hop in my car and I'll take you along as I go home," smiled Nankivell and he rose, stretched himself, bade the man on duty in the charge room goodnight and followed his men out into the darkness.

10

ENTER A GANGSTER

About nine o'clock next morning, Nankivell resumed work. He felt bleary-eyed from last night's late sitting and his mouth was like dry blotting-paper from overmuch smoking. A day in the country would just have suited him, with something to wet his whistle on the way, and he decided to visit the searchlight camp as soon as possible. Patchett, marvellously none-the-worse, was already afield collecting alibis and hoped to save himself a journey to Moggridge's farm at Leather Lea to confirm Burt's statement, by catching the old farmer at the weekly cattle-market, still held in Swarebridge, although in an attenuated form.

Nankivell was just turning over the last of his morning's post preparatory to sallying out, when a disturbance arose in the porch of the police station.

A shrill, childish voice alternating with that of an angry and bothered woman.

"You're comin' in, I tell you, and tellin' Mr Nankivell wot you 'eard…"

"Aw. I don't wanna. I ain't a stool-pigeon."

"You *what?*" The woman's voice rose in a shrill interrogative crescendo.

"I ain't squealin'!"

"You'd better not try squealing or yellin'. Won't do you no good. You got to tell your tale, or I'll set your father on you again and you know wot that'll mean..."

"Third-degree wiv the buckle-end of his belt agen," came the prompt, unflinching reply.

"Don't talk none o' your geometry to me. If this is what education does to you..."

The Superintendent opened the door just in time to receive in his arms the figure of a small, chubby, sulky-looking boy propelled by a furious maternal shove.

"There. Look wot you done you...you... Oh, put 'im in the lock-up, Mr Nankivell. I can't do no good with 'im."

"I ain't goin' in no cooler," said the urchin, his voice pitched in a lower, less defiant key, with almost a trace of tears in the offing.

The turbulent newcomer was Cuthbert Silversides, aged nine. The name of Cuthbert was anathema to him, and among his associates he was known as Spider. Why, no one knew, except that young Silversides chose it for himself after a visit to the pictures. For Cuthbert was a gangster. He was the leading light of a small unruly crowd of Mr Hewston's boys, whose high spirits led them into all kinds of behaviour which they imagined to be lawless and daring. To their elders, however, it was sometimes amusing, more often a nuisance, but invariably on the right side of the fence. Their education hitherto had been mainly in the hands of Mr Truscott, manager of the local picture-house, who illicitly allowed them to sneak-in to see his "A" films. Cuthbert's boyish prattle was liberally interspersed with juicy phrases from one-time Chicago vocabulary. Theoretically, he was against the police. Standing now before Nankivell, he had his doubts.

Mrs Silversides, the tired-looking, hard-working wife of one of Pogsley's electricians and mother of three more younger than "Spider," was unwashed and a bit dishevelled, as though, hearing of her son's adventures, she had risen straight from bed, flung on her garments and rushed him off to confess. Holding him tightly by the back of his jersey, she poured out a breathless rigmarole to the Superintendent.

Cuthbert (the boy winced at the very sound of it!), Cuthbert was at the school party on Saturday, having walked in the procession in his new clothes, which he'd made in a shocking mess through rifling a box belonging to the dramatic society and making himself up to look like what he thought was *The Face at the Window* or something. (Cuthbert writhed again as this compliment passed over his head, for he had never met *Le Loup*, the most terrible criminal in his mother's scanty repertory.) Yes, Cuthbert was at the party. But he wasn't at chapel the day after, nor at school on Monday, nor at the meeting at Sunday school later.

"… And you tell the gentleman why," wound-up the mother, furiously shaking the captive in the jersey, until that garment slid round his neck and almost choked him.

"I was sick," feebly said the boy.

"Go on! Tell 'im wot for. It'll teach you next time. Tell 'im."

"Well?" said Nankivell, itching to end the interview and get about his job, but maintaining a smiling face and standing, arms akimbo, before the gangster.

"I pinched a pot of lemon cheese from Sunday School kitchen and ate it. Then I was sick," replied the youngster, and as if the last event were a source of pride, he perked-up wonderfully.

Mrs Silversides then added that Cuthbert was given castor oil on the Sunday and couldn't be trusted out on Monday in consequence.

"But I went to the meetin' last night," continued his mother, smacking her lips. "Shockin'! 'Orrible! Not safe to stir out of doors, it isn't. Well, as I was sayin', I went and after it was over, I went 'ome and told me 'usband all about everythin'. Good job our Cuthbert was at 'ome, sez he, else it might 'ave been 'im, instead of pore Willie. Well, as we wuz talkin', his lordship," here she again shook the jersey, "'is lordship, who's crep' downstairs and is listenin' behind the door, sneezes, so my 'usband catches 'im and threatens to tan the hide off 'im for bein' out o' bed. Then, if you please, the little divil up and tells his dad he knows somethin' about wot old 'Arbuttle did on Saturday, but 'e wasn't tellin' the police..."

"I ain't a squealer," said a muffled voice from the jersey.

"Nobody said you woz, and don't give me enny of yer lip. His father's the only one who can handle his lordship properly. He made 'im tell. Now, *you*, tell the gentleman and don't miss any of it, or I'll box yer ears..."

Either the spate of his mother's talk was getting on his nerves or the way in which she punctuated her discourse was demoralising the gangster, for he began to snivel.

"I didn't do nothin'. You ain't got nuttin' on me," he whined.

"Tell 'im..." came inexorably from the mother.

"I was only gettin' some acid-drops from me maw's pocket..."

"Gettin'? Stealin's the word...a week's ration for all the family...and after I'd queued an hour to get 'em... Go on, you young monkey!"

"They was in my maw's pocket in the mothers' classroom and I went to get one..."

"One!! Not if I knows you..."

"When I got to the classroom there was somebody in. The door was shut... I opened it... Mr 'Arbuttle and somebody else was there talkin'... Mr 'Arbuttle sez to me 'Wot you wantin'?'

'Me mother's coat,' I sez. 'You be off, quick, and don't disturb me,' 'e sez. So I went."

Nankivell looked keenly at the boy. His tale seemed to ring true.

"Who was with him, Cuthbert?" he asked.

"I couldn't see the other guy…"

"'Oo?"

"The other chap…"

"That's better…"

"The other chap was behind the door, and Mr 'Arbuttle 'eld it as he spoke. Then 'e shut it in me face."

"Did you hear anything of what was said, Cuthbert?"

"I went an' disguised myself and came back. They was still there, and I listened outside and I 'eard old 'Arbuttle…"

"'Oo?"

"*Mister* 'Arbuttle say to the other g-chap, 'You gotta come clean to the p'lice and right now and take your medicine like a man. Else, when I see Nankivell tonight, I'll give 'im the works meself…"

"'E never said that!" furiously interjected the mother. "'e never said that! H'alderman 'Arbuttle never talked like that. 'E hadn't 'ad the fancy schoolin' yor gettin'. Where you pick it up from, I *do not* know. These central schools…" She trailed-off apologetically.

Nankivell almost burst internally, suppressing his mirth.

Cuthbert the Spider had recovered his poise somewhat but was overawed in the presence of the real law. He fixed his eyes on a glass case filled with a collection of out-of-date gyves collected by the Chief Constable and presented to the Force, which didn't in the least appreciate the gift on account of the cleaning involved by it.

"Are them 'andcuffs…bracelets…?" he whispered.

"Yes," replied the Superintendent and seizing the awed gangster under the armpits, he lifted him high enough for inspection.

In the twinkling of an eye, Cuthbert (Spider) Silversides was converted into a G-Man.

* * *

ON HIS WAY to the camp Nankivell pondered the problem over the driving-wheel.

Someone had to take his medicine and Harbuttle was seeing to it that he did so. So, the unknown silenced Harbuttle, but, rightly or wrongly, thought that Willie Pole had seen him choosing his weapon. So poor Willie had to die.

Who had Harbuttle caught out? Had Butterfield been swindling the company? Or, had Singleton been at something shady? Or the parson? Or...oh, damn it all, it might be anybody. The kid had overheard it, or said he'd overheard it, just after tea. Harbuttle must have been hunting for his victim and buttonholed him on the first opportunity. What about? The best thing seemed to be to go steadily on investigating as planned, although so far, there wasn't a sign of who'd done it. Couldn't question the whole town! Looked like a Scotland Yard job after all. But what could the Yard do with so many possibilities...?

The car mounted steadily, drawing nearer to the ancient earthwork so convenient for a searchlight station. A very short distance from the pleasant ring of trees which surrounded the mound was established a busy colony of men in charge of the plant. About eight privates and a corporal; two or three of them actual technicians, the rest engaged in cooking, guard duty, observation and storekeeping. Nankivell greeted the sentry and asked to see the officer in charge. He found the corporal busy writing in a wooden hut amid the smell of cooking from the nearby kitchen. He explained his business at once.

"Oh, there are several of them very interested in what goes on around, and they spend hours a day when there's nothing more exciting to occupy their minds, in watching what's happening here and there. Higgins is the most talkative of the lot, however. He seems to have an eye for outlandish things. I'll find him. He's cleaning the generator."

The corporal left and shortly returned with a stocky, whimsical-looking private in a soiled suit of dungarees. He had twinkling dark eyes and an inquisitive look and settled down to business with relish.

"Oh, yes, I sees quite a lot o' goings-on when I'm on dooty. Them glasses is top-hole. Brings the object right on your front doorstep, so to speak," said Higgins.

Nankivell pointed out the towers of Pisgah in the distance.

"Do you ever take a good look at the house, the one with the funny towers there, for example?"

"You betcha. There's a cove there takes as much interest in us as we do in him. Not been so busy lately, but we'll be seein' him again, sure as eggs is eggs."

"I'm afraid you won't. He was murdered last Saturday."

"Corblimey! You don't say? Poor old bloke."

"Yes. That's why I'm here. There's a bit of a mystery about the old chap's death and I'd like you to tell me all you know, or all you've seen there."

"Not much, guvnor. I fancy what started 'im watching us first was the girls as used to come up here flirtin' with the boys, like. You know, guvnor, always a few bits o' skirt hangin' round a soldier, eh? Well, when the boys is off duty, some of 'em enjoys a bit o' canoodlin' and a bit o' sport on the hillside here. The old chap must a' spotted 'em and got busy with his glasses. Seat in the dress-circle, as you might say. When I found out — spotted 'im through me own glasses — when I found out, I tipped the lad the wink, like, and they went Don Jewonning on the other side o' the 'ill where the old fellow couldn't watch 'em."

"Hm. Anything else?"

"Well, he seemed kinder interested in all that went on. Used ter watch us up here, friendly like. I've put me 'and up to 'im, greetin' like, and he's waved back. But he watched the road, too, as far as I could see. A good look-out, he 'ad, and the reverse of this place, as you might say. We're on one side o' the valley, he's on the ovver. He saw the front door and we saw the back of what went on, see?"

"Yes. Anything interesting that took your eyes, that might have appealed to the old chap, too?"

"Oh, all sorts. Lovin' couples, speed 'ogs on the road, cattle and things in fields for them as likes that sort o' thing, and comings and goings at those three farms there."

He pointed to the farmsteads, two prosperous, large establishments on either side of Doyle's Farm, the latter known locally as Toad-in-Hole.

"Them two, on each side, like," said Higgins, pointing to the larger ones, "Them two is always busy. Sheep, cattle, labourers, land girls. Proper back-to-the-land, dig-for-victory places. But the one between 'em's as quiet as the grave. By day, that is. At night, it livens up a bit."

"What do you mean?"

"Come 'ere."

Private Higgins took Nankivell to the gate of the camp, where the sentry stood watching the skies with his field-glasses.

"Lend us yer glasses, Bert," went on the little man, and taking them from his pal, he fixed them on Toad-in-Hole.

"Like the grave. Not a thing. Teck a look."

Nankivell did as he was bidden. The place looked deserted. Untidy buildings. A large manure heap in the yard. The door of the house closed and no smoke from the chimneys. He remembered that Doyle, the tenant, had, before the Ministry restrictions, been a cattle dealer. In fact, he'd come from Ireland for that express purpose and had let-off the fifty or so acres attached to his farm to his neighbours, using the place merely as a residence and depot for his livestock. Now, he seemed simply to live in the house and do very little business at the weekly mart. It was Tuesday, cattle-market day, which perhaps explained why the farm was neglected and closed.

"Hm," said the Superintendent, handing back the glasses. "Not much doing."

"Get busy some nights, though. Every now and then, we practise with the light." Higgins pointed over his shoulder to the apparatus, set in its own miniature earthwork on the hill. "Lights up the countryside like moonlight, you know. Well, sometimes when it's turned on over the direction of the town, it's nearly a limelight over the country around. And two or three times, we've been able to see that farm there, busy, as you might say. Men comin' and goin' out and in sheds, carryin' things, and once driving cows out of a van into the cowsheds."

Nankivell scratched his chin thoughtfully.

"That's interesting," he said. "Wonder what it was. Perhaps Doyle moving cattle for somebody. I remember, a large part of his trade used to be cattle transport. He's two big motor-vans for the purpose."

"But why allus at night, guvnor? Sounds like a bit o' jiggery-pokery to me. Perhaps a bit o' meat off the ration, so to speak."

The shrewd little soldier looked up at the police officer and winked. Nankivell had just been thinking the same. This would bear investigating. Suppose Harbuttle had seen them...

"I wonder if the old man saw anything of this," Nankivell uttered his thoughts aloud...

"Like as not," replied Higgins. "Not so much that old cuss'd miss. Perhaps he spotted somethin' and poked 'is nose a bit too far in it. Now, if a chap like me, with his duties to do and kep' busy, like, can spot and put two and two together, same as I just told you, surely the old un, with all day to play about in, might a seen more. *And* he knew everybody concerned. Not like me, a stranger to the place."

"Well, our talk's been very useful, Mr Higgins, and I'm very much obliged to you. If you're ever lonely or thirsty when you're in town, just call on the police and we'll see what we can do about it. Goodbye."

"S'long, sir. I'll be seein' yer in a day or two. Not 'arf."

Higgins licked his lips, spat cheerfully, and returned to his engines.

11

TOAD-IN-HOLE FARM

The remainder of Tuesday was discouraging to Nankivell. The inquest on Harbuttle was held after lunch, and by arrangement between the police and the coroner, was merely formal and was adjourned *sine die* after ten minutes' proceedings. This greatly disappointed the audience which crowded the coroner's court to suffocation and those assembled murmured against Mr Ishmael Knott, the officer in question, for not giving them more entertainment. Seditious utterances such as "What did he want sittin' without a jury? 'Tain't legal if you ask me," and "Couldn't a-been suicide, now could it? Oughter returned verdict o' murder agen person or persons unknowed," were freely bandied about and it was hinted by more than one that Mr Knott didn't know his job properly. The coroner, however, didn't care a hoot about the talk. By rights, Tuesday was his afternoon off, and he was delighted at the brevity of Harbuttle's requirements. He hurried off forthwith to the country, where he had some rough-shooting, and what he lacked in furred and feathered victims, he made up in noise and empty cartridge cases.

Nankivell was, as we have said, discouraged. Patchett, after slogging round in the hope of finding one of his list with a vulnerable alibi, returned to report that there was nothing suspicious. Mr Butterfield, for example, rallied three undoubted witnesses to the fact that whilst he was querulous and protesting concerning the violation of the chapel by followers of my leader, he did not break ranks. The three clubmen on the list, too, all proved that whilst the crime was being committed, they were watching a sensational game of snooker at the Constitutional. They had about twenty-five witnesses to fall back on and there was not a flaw in their case. Moggridge had given Burt his alibi, too, in a shrill, cantankerous bellow, uttered above similar noises in the heart of the cattle-market. Only Singleton of the bunch of anaemic suspects had been unable to fence himself in. He and his wife, both of them engaged in trying to get 120 one-pound packets out of a hundredweight of tea, were wild at the idea that the grocer should be suspected of trying to hurry the process of nature by polishing-off Harbuttle. They vehemently asserted that long before the crime, Singleton was sitting before his own fireside, with his slippers on his feet and a cup of cocoa at his elbow, reading the current copy of *The Good News*, a weekly to which he was particularly addicted. It was coming to something if a man had to have strangers in his home whenever he wanted a quiet five minutes, just in case somebody should get murdered in the cold world outside and he might have to get himself an alibi! Patchett gave it up and placed a question mark beside Singleton's name in his note-book. That symbol did not mean that the grocer was suspect, however, for Patchett was later heard to remark that Singleton hadn't the guts to murder a rice pudding, which was a shrewd, if obscure comment.

Nankivell, after receiving the Inspector's report, decided to leave theorising for the time being and make a trip to Toad-in-Hole Farm. There was something going on there which called for enquiry, if Higgins's tale was to be credited, and whether events were in any way connected with Harbuttle or not, nothing would be lost by the journey. Especially, as it was through pretty country and Nankivell was fond of walking. Judging that by this time, Doyle would have returned from the market, the Superintendent lighted his pipe and set off at a swinging pace for the farm.

From the highway a rough cart-track led down to Doyle's place which from the distance, looked still to be silent and deserted. The main gate sagged and creaked on its rusty hinges, the courtyard of the house would have been better for a good shower of rain or a few buckets of water, the garden was a wilderness of nettles and one-time domestic plants now gone wild. The whole establishment savoured of neglect and decay. The stables were empty, the cowsheds quiet and forlorn, hen-runs, untenanted, were tumbled about, their timbers rotting and their wire rusty and in gaping holes. Only the barn of all the outbuildings seemed in use. From the oil and tyre marks around, Nankivell judged that it was used for Doyle's cattle-vans. He turned to the farmhouse, the windows of which were covered inside by cheap and filthy muslin curtains and looked as if they had not been cleaned since the Irishman took over. The door was locked, and there was no sign of life indoors. The Superintendent knew that Doyle fended for himself domesti-cally, obtaining such feminine company as he craved from the lower parts of the town or the beer houses. A simpleton, Lot Wilkins, was handyman, and Nankivell hunted round for him. He was nowhere to be seen. Apparently played truant in the absence of his master! Nankivell clicked his tongue against his teeth in disgust at the sight of a once cosy little holding now tumbledown and spoiled. He turned to leave the place until later but gave a final peep into the nearest outbuildings. Dust and filth everywhere, rotting mangers, rusty iron, decaying sacks and old harness. To add to the general air of unpleasantness, a large heap of stale manure in the centre of the farmyard gave forth unsavoury odours and swarms of flies. Nankivell contemplated this thoughtfully. The centre of the noisome mass had apparently been recently disturbed. If Doyle kept no stock, whence the dung; why disturb it if not cultivating fields or garden? There might have been some good reason, but the officer was intrigued. He turned to find some fork or other implement, but none was to hand. He decided to try the farm buildings again.

The Superintendent thrust his head in one after another of the cowsheds and stables but found nothing he could use for his purpose. At length, he came to an isolated byre, tucked away in a corner, probably, in days past, used as a quiet spot for calving cows or such. The door was secured by a chain and padlock. Nankivell shook the latter and it opened in his hand, apparently having been half-locked in haste, or else got out-of-gear from use. Entering, he found a place very different from elsewhere. The cobbled floor was spotless and had the appearance of being frequently swilled. The walls were whitewashed. A stiff broom, a spade and a fork were leaning against one wall, in which was also fastened a number of staples with chains, such as are used for securing cattle.

Nankivell pushed his hat back on his head, stood with his hands on his hips and contemplated this unexpected scene. Closely he examined the cobblestones on the floor, prodded the earth between them with the prongs of the fork and grunted. He took a sample of this on the end of a flat stick, placed it in an envelope and pocketed it. At length, he took the fork, strode to the manure heap and turned over the freshly disturbed portions. At some depth he halted, held his breath, stooped and carefully inspected the contents of the hole he had made. He grunted again and screwed up his nose. The mess of putrid flesh before him, combined with the traces of fresh dung and coagulated blood he had found on the floor of the cowshed, confirmed his original vague suspicions. Doyle was running an illegal slaughterhouse on his farm and presumably carrying on black-marketing of butcher's meat!

Nankivell levelled-up the dunghill again, restored the fork, closed the byre and washed his hands at a ramshackle cattle-trough. As he dried them on his handkerchief, he heard shambling footsteps approaching. Lot Wilkins turned the corner and entered the yard. He halted as he saw Nankivell and stood regarding the interloper, his loose mouth open, his small weak eyes showing a mixture of cunning and fear, his bullet-shaped head lolling.

"Hullo, Wilkins. Where've you been and where's Doyle?" asked Nankivell.

Lot Wilkins considered for a minute, as though allowing the words to sink in his dim brain and convey some meaning. He had a cleft palate and spoke with difficulty. He tried to answer at length, his mouth working. He raised his chin and struggled to articulate.

"Gone off…off…away…" he said, his face contorted as if each word seared his tongue.

"Where?"

"Away…gone off…" repeated the man with the same convulsions.

Nankivell turned and regarded the house. Locked up. Perhaps Doyle had packed-up and taken himself off. There was a ladder lying under one of the walls. This Nankivell raised to one of the bedroom windows and mounted aloft. Rubbing off a circle of dirt from one of the panes with his hand, the Superintendent peered in. The room was empty save for a few old sticks of furniture and bundles of rubbish. He moved the ladder to the next window and repeated his operations. This time he found himself looking into a bedroom, evidently Doyle's quarters. Squalid, with a dirty, dishevelled bed and a piece or two of cheap bedroom furniture. The drawers, however, took the officer's eye. They had been removed bodily and their contents strewn about. The place was a shambles. Old clothes and personal articles scattered here and there, apparently left by someone hastily packing.

So Doyle had fled! Why? Nankivell remembered Higgins's tale and his suspicions that Harbuttle had perhaps, like the soldier himself, discovered some tiddley-boodley going on at the farm. Had Harbuttle challenged Doyle? And had Doyle silenced him and fled?

Surely, however, the Irishman, who never saw the inside of a church, would never have made a rendezvous in a classroom at Zion. All the same, in desperation, he might have done anything. Fines were stiff and imprisonment long for this kind of thing nowadays and a hot-tempered, unscrupulous rascal like Doyle might stop at nothing. Better take steps to lay the fugitive by the heels at once.

Nankivell hastily replaced the ladder. Lot Wilkins was struggling to speak, but the Superintendent did not stay to listen. The labourer seemed rooted to the spot and Nankivell left him there, his feet gently marking time, his head lolling, his mouth dribbling and his dim, gentle blue eyes questioning and vacant as those of a very little child.

12

MUTINY OF A PARSON

The Reverend B Augustus Partington looked at his engagement-pad and thrust it from him in disgust. Two funerals, including that of Harbuttle, and a wedding. Net increment, twenty-five bob. Suddenly realising what he was thinking, counting up the brides and corpses in terms of £ s d, the poor fellow gazed forlornly round the cold little room he called his study, and then buried his head in his hands. He was so depressed that he felt like making a beast of himself on the small, sealed bottle of brandy, providently laid by in the ARP first-aid kit by Mrs Partington. In his agony, he rebelled against the God he served.

"Why pick on me?" he mutinously asked a discoloured spot on the ceiling.

As the doorbell rang, he wondered what next.

Of late, his nerves had gone to pieces through mental and physical wrestling with sin, doubt and the family budget.

In college, the head of young Partington was in the clouds. He saw bright visions of the Kingdom on earth. He was Moses on a different kind of Pisgah from old Harbuttle's motley mountain of yellow bricks and white mortar, and his Canaan was pleasant to the eye. He was fired by the joy of his calling and stood with his spiritual sleeves rolled up for the fray which he hoped any day to join. He would have brushed aside as pagan, superstitious claptrap any suggestion that the gods were jealous. All the same, at the height of his elation, they were preparing a number of surprises for him. Over a period of eighteen months he failed his BA, he married, he received a call to Zion, he found himself involved in an outrageous scandal and, finally, two of his flock were foully done to death and he was by way of being a suspect himself!

The BA, of course, was just too bad. He over-studied in his enthusiasm, suffered a complete breakdown in the examination room, wrote an essay worthy of Voltaire himself on certain articles of faith, and was only rescued from expulsion from College by a psychoanalyst who was also a member of the governing body. His nervous condition was a blessing in disguise, however, when, a month or two later, he began to hunt for his first job. His preaching was so full of intense and burning fervour, due to increased, almost morbid sensitivity, that he received a "call" from Swarebridge Zion Chapel at once. This filled his fellow students with envy, for Zion was described as a "plum" of the denomination. The young parson was full of hope and zest, but whilst his head was in the clouds, his feet grew very vulnerable. That wealthy church valued its pastor at a mere three hundred pounds a year and on it Mrs Partington could not make ends meet.

Here we see him then, with Nankivell ringing his front doorbell, a fledgling minister, sitting in the ashes of his hopes, as the Victorians would say. Temporary ashes, of course, for we know that the phoenix leaps from temperaments like that of Partington. One day, some university will make up for the lost BA by an honorary DD. He will become a leader of his denomination. At worst, he'll find his level, either calmly and deliberately with shattering cynicism, or through a revelation, a brainstorm. Then, squashed and moulded afresh by circumstances, his spirit will grow quiet and he will settle down as must many others of his cloth, to a job instead of a mission.

Partington looked at Nankivell apprehensively as he opened the door and discovered who had been ringing.

"Good evening, Superintendent. Won't you come in?"

"Good evening, Mr Partington. Yes. I'd like a word or two with you if you can spare a minute. I won't keep you long."

He followed the minister down the long corridor to his study. The hall was furnished in heavy furniture, with third-rate oil paintings on the walls. An old-fashioned, rambling place, the last of its line on the main street and fully equipped by Pogsley when purchased for Zion. The study was a small, book-lined room. Two sides were covered by ponderous tomes, the sermons of long-forgotten divines, concordances, commentaries, bound volumes of religious journals, devotional books. Another Pogsley endowment. The parson's own meagre library filled a few small shelves beneath the window. A mixed lot of moderns this time, with here and there something in lighter vein. Hobhouse, Leacock, Henri Bergson, Aldous Huxley, Cadoux, Richard Aldington, William James, Anatole France, and a number of schoolboy volumes of algebra, geometry and Latin. Pogsley would have turned in his mausoleum had he known of some of them!

The two men drew up to a large desk in the middle of the room. The fire burned brightly. There were the remnants of a scratch meal on a tray on the floor. Partington swept aside a number of books and papers, leaned his elbows wearily across his blotting pad and looked enquiringly at his visitor.

"Well, Superintendent, I've been expecting you."

"Why, sir?"

This took the wind out of the parson's sails. He gave no answer and Nankivell tactfully did not press the point.

"I called for a general discussion with you, Mr Partington. As head of the church, you will probably have some valuable help to give me; something which might throw a light on the present problems."

"I'm sure I'll help all I can, although I can't see how."

"Well, in the first place, let's deal with your own personal movements on Saturday night. Monday doesn't matter; you were with me during the terrible happenings then. Will you begin by telling me what you did on Saturday evening?"

Partington jumped nervously at the question and began to speak at once.

"I left well before nine with Mr Wildbore. We were off to the station to meet Dr Cowslip on the nine thirty-three from London. It was to time; we took the doctor to Wildbore's place — he was staying the night there — and then I returned to the school. I got there somewhere just after ten. Wildbore will bear me out on that point."

"He's already done so, Mr Partington. Don't have any apprehension on that score. You've a good alibi, even if you were suspect, which you aren't."

The minister's face cleared. He had a genuine regard for Nankivell, was a welcome visitor in his home from time to time, and always got a cordial reception there.

"*You* didn't by any chance see anyone suspicious hanging round the knives in the kitchen, I suppose?"

"No, Superintendent. I'm afraid I was busy right from arriving at tea until I left for the station."

"Yet, I understood you to say you overheard Harbuttle proposing to Miss Arrowsmith in the course of the evening. Is that so?"

Partington was plunged into confusion. He turned alternately pale and dull-pink and looked anywhere but at the man addressing him.

"That's not quite true, Superintendent," he whispered at length, his voice husky and seeming to come from a long distance. "I *did* know of it. I was getting my hat and coat from the passage outside the classrooms, when I came across Singleton in a furious temper. He was talking to himself angrily and as I was the only one about, he vented his spleen on me. 'What do you think's the latest?' he said, livid with fury. 'Our old chap's just proposing to a girl young enough to be his grand-daughter. Muriel Arrowsmith. He's gone mad ...'"

"Yes. Was that all?"

The minister hesitated. There was something more, but he was finding it hard to get it off his chest. He nervously clutched his cheek as though struggling to hold in his words and puffed into his hand.

"Come, come, sir. You can talk to me in confidence. We're friends, you know. Anything you tell me will be strictly between ourselves, unless, of course, the ends of justice demand that it be made public."

A feeling of intense relief surged over the parson's spirit. The big, friendly police officer gave him confidence. He felt he had few real friends in Zion. He was expected, as pastor, to hear secrets and distil comfort for others, but he could open his heart to very few, if any, of those who would surely whisper his secrets abroad or look upon them as undermining his prestige. His repressed thoughts burst forth in a torrent of words.

"He said, Singleton said... 'And she's your bit o' stuff, eh?' Most offensively. An abominable thought and a wicked lie, not only believed by Singleton, but by many others. There's scandalous talk going on in Zion about me and Miss Arrowsmith. Never, in thought or deed, have I been untrue to my wife. I swear it. I seem to have got entangled in some sort of a ghastly nightmare conspiracy to take away my good name. So much so, that my wife, who's expecting a baby, has almost broken down under the vile business. Whispering, and even plain-speaking, as some of the harpies call it, smacking their lips. I've sent her away to her mother's and, and...well, I might as well tell you, I'm canvassing for a new church. I couldn't bear our child to be born here under this cloud."

"Didn't you have words with the late Mr Harbuttle on that subject, Mr Partington?" interjected Nankivell.

"So, you've heard of it, too? Who hasn't?" replied the minister in despair.

"You must forgive my bringing this unpleasant topic into the conversation, but you'll appreciate that anything involving the victim is now the business of the police."

Partington winced.

"Yes. Alderman Harbuttle had a strange mind. He was fond of the young ladies himself, but, being a widower, seemed under the impression that his fancy could rove wherever he wished it. Others, however, weren't allowed such licence. He *did* mention it to me. I told him it was a monstrous insinuation and that at the next full meeting of deacons, I would bring it forward myself, if *he* didn't, and if he didn't publicly recant, they'd have to look for another minister."

"Was that all?"

"Yes. I'll admit I was friendly with the Arrowsmiths, but I wasn't calling on the daughter. I like Arrowsmith, himself. He's a bit of a character. Straightforward and a bit lonely. We got on fine. I've taken Muriel home a time or two after choir rehearsals, but that's been when I've been calling on the old chap. My wife knew all about it…"

"Perhaps the girl took it more seriously than you did."

"Why? I'm married, am I not…?"

"Yes, but you know how the folk whose be-all and end-all is the church seem to get in a groove of narrow-mindedness. You can't be too careful, can you?"

"No. When I left college, Dr Cowslip warned me what to expect, but in my own mind I thought him a bit of an old fossil. He was right. When I came here, I'd just got engaged. I had to make a hurried marriage of it, by Jove, or else some of the eligible virgins of the place would have had me! It's incredible."

"Yes, it's rather an old story, isn't it? Your professor was wise and experienced."

"Well, I've been through the mill since I came here. They're very decent people, taken as a whole, but too critical and exacting. One's life isn't one's own..."

"A parson can hardly expect that, can he? He's like a doctor, and all other public servants..."

"Oh, yes. But there are limits."

"Yes. But to return to the business of my call. Is there anything concerning Harbuttle and his recent doings that you think might help us in the investigation of this crime? You'll realise that the murder of little Willie Pole is more or less a corollary of the first one; find one, and the other will be solved as a matter of course, I think."

"I'm sorry, Superintendent. I can't think of a thing. None of the domestic quarrels of Zion is sufficient to cause a murder. Besides, that's not the Christian way out, nor the Zion way out, either. Don't you agree?"

"Yes, I think I do."

"And you're no nearer a solution?"

"Not much. We're following up one or two threads and I hope one or the other of them will lead us somewhere."

A sharp snapping sound in a cupboard by the fire made the minister jump almost out of his skin.

"Mice?" said Nankivell rising to take his leave.

"Yes. The place is overrun with them. I hate having to set traps, but what can one do?"

The poor man looked so distressed that the Superintendent felt heartily sorry for him. He seemed tossed hither and thither without much of an anchor. Nankivell remembered Partington's struggles and experiments since his first arrival, a newly ordained parson, at Zion. He seemed to be continually riding some favourite horse. A man of many enthusiasms. Like a fire of burning twigs; all flame and no heat and subsiding quickly. New Thought, Groups, Boy Scouts, what Hewston had called "Shower Baths in the Infinite," and finally, even psychoanalysis. Partington had tried them all. Poor chap. He was a long time in choosing the tools of his trade. Nankivell felt glad that he was a policeman. After all, he had rules and regulations and a cut-and-dried technique; Partington had his faith, a flickering flame, likely to be extinguished by heaven-knew-what douche or breeze of fate. A rotten job these days and calling for every ounce of grit and fortitude.

"Look here," said Nankivell as he shook the parson's hand at the door. "We're always glad to see you for a meal at our place. Don't make yourself ill by neglecting your stomach or eating too much out of tins. And above all, don't sit here brooding. Everything will come out all right. I hope you soon get a good job and you and your wife will be happy and settled when the time comes."

Partington almost broke down and promised to call soon and often.

Nankivell strolled to the police station in the gathering darkness. The streets were deserted. Even the picture-houses seemed to be having a thin time. People were staying at home. Two murders in three days had scared the good people of Swarebridge. A strange foreboding hung over the place. In the pubs, pianos were playing, and drunken shouts could be heard. The topers were gathering liquid courage and would see each other home for safety after turning-out time…

At the police station the sergeant on duty saluted his chief and bade him good evening.

"Any news of Doyle?" asked Nankivell, turning over the papers on the desk.

"No, sir. There's hardly been time yet. They'll be on the look-out at stations and ports. They'll get him, sure as my name's Pettigrew."

"Yes, I suppose they will. If any news comes through, ring me up at home, sergeant."

"What? Waken you up, sir?"

"Yes. You'd better. I'll feel happier when we have him. Although what good it's going to do, I don't know, I can hardly imagine Doyle choosing a chapel for a murder. However... Goodnight, sergeant."

"Goodnight, sir."

Sergeant Pettigrew looked puzzled, blew into his red moustache, shook his head and listened carefully until his chief's footsteps had faded away in the distance. Then he took a paper-backed wild-west novel from his drawer and ponderously immersed himself in it.

"Oh, 'ell," said Sergeant Pettigrew as the telephone jangled. He marked his place in the book with a thick forefinger and contorted himself into a listening posture.

"Swarebridge police station," he said in what he thought was the terse manner employed by the sheriff of Four Horse Gulch.

A voice began to speak. Sergeant Pettigrew's eyes grew wider, his moustache bristled, and his mouth slowly opened.

"Well, well, well," he gasped. He could not think of anything else to say.

13

PASTRYCOOK'S DILEMMA

On the fateful Monday evening which saw the death of little Willie Pole and the terrible battle of women in Zion, Mr Axel Adolf Meister, Swiss pastrycook, began his nocturnal task of making tomorrow's bread and other bake-meats. It was his habit to labour all through the night at his boards and ovens, skilfully struggling to overcome war-time rations and make the best of such limited supplies as came his way. This he did greatly to the satisfaction of the women of Swarebridge, whom he could see in long queues waiting for opening time as he paused in setting out his window and peeped through a chink in the blind. Nine o'clock saw the shop door opened. Customers surged in like ravening locusts and by ten o'clock had swept the place clean, leaving nothing behind but crumbs, bits of paper, and a few packets of unsweetened biscuits which hadn't taken well with the public. Then, the last of the jostling throng having departed, Mr Meister retired to the room behind the shop, ate his breakfast, or supper, whichever you like, and retired to bed leaving his wife to send the late-comers empty away.

Meister was a small, portly man with a pink, bald, Teutonic

head, innocent blue eyes, a bulbous nose and a large fair moustache. His complexion had the sunless, waxen hue characteristic of many who work by night and sleep by day, but his heart was warm and kind and whilst to outsiders he might appear grave and thoughtful, to his intimate circle he was a jocular and cultured companion. His English wife and two daughters adored him. These three were British nationals; father remained Swiss. He had promised his mother, still alive and healthy in Herzogenbuchsee, Canton Berne, that he would not change and now, above all times, when he had not seen her for four years through the marooning of his homeland, he could not go back on her. He was no neutral, however, and over a period of seven years had entirely suppressed his second Christian name.

We meet Mr Axel Meister, then, in his bed at four o'clock on Tuesday afternoon. He has not slept since he retired from his locust-swept shop. The duvet, his wife's concession to native custom, lies on the floor, a shapeless mass. The bedclothes of the huge four-poster are tangled and knotted. The gentle eyes of Mr Meister are wide open and his proud moustache droops petulantly. Under his eyes are dark puffy circles of sleeplessness. His fat fingers clutch the clothes up to his chin and fidget ceaselessly. Over his head hangs a framed text: *Eine feste Burg ist unser Gott.* Mr Meister attends no place of religion, having been brought up strict Lutheran at home. He is wrestling with his conscience now.

The trouble is that this morning in the shop, Mr Meister heard that last night Superintendent Nankivell was enquiring if anyone had seen suspicious goings-on in the kitchens of Zion on the previous Saturday evening. The pastrycook, as official caterer, had much to do with that department, and although not one of the anniversary revellers, he had passed to and from Zion bearing loaves and quantities of his excellent flat jam-cakes, native dishes of Herzogenbuchsee readily adopted by Swarebridge. Calling for his empty trays on the evening of the crime,

Mr Meister had seen the hindquarters of a well-known citizen of the town disappearing from the otherwise deserted canteen at the time suggested by the police. Conflicting emotions struggled in the little man's breast and deprived him of sleep.

On the one hand, Meister was a great admirer of Nankivell. As a Swiss national, the baker had periodically to report himself to the police. He knew countries on the Continent where, even in brighter days, such procedure was an ordeal and where to be an alien reporting his whereabouts was akin to being on ticket-of-leave. The suspicious looks, the patronage, the scorn were hardly worth the sojourn. Here, however, the pastrycook almost looked forward to dropping-in Swarebridge police station. He could enter smoking his pipe, holding high his head. They greeted him cheerfully and as an equal. Nay, in their hospitality, they were as solicitous as a hen over her chickens. Especially Nankivell. Nothing was too much trouble. Not that Meister needed anything. After more than thirty years, he felt quite at home. But there it was. The police were his intimate friends. Even thirty-odd years ago, when he arrived in London with nothing but a dictionary of phrases to guide him, he had pointed out one of them to a policeman: "Where can I get a room for the night?" And then, "Can you place me in contact with anyone who is Swiss?" And the bobby had answered both queries in a most practical manner and given him his start in this new land he was adopting. Yes, the police had always been his friends. He ought to tell them what he knew. It wasn't as easy as that, however.

Mr Meister was a musician. He played the cello and around him he had gathered a string quartet. His eldest daughter, first violin; Tilly Burt, second violin (she played it far better than the organ); Stanley Butterfield, viola; and himself on the cello. Next week, Percy Wildbore, son of the JP, was joining them with his cello and they were to make a start at Schubert's Quintet for strings in C. For years Meister had been hunting for a second cellist for this purpose. His heart was set on it. In these days more than ever, music lightened his soul's dark places. He lusted for it as an addict craves for his drugs. Not only that; it bound him to the rest of his little group of players with silver cords. They were so happy together, so friendly and intimate. Over coffee and his special pastries afterwards, they were so merry, so cheerful together. Now, he could fling a bombshell in their midst and destroy the joyful unions for good. Meister tossed and turned. He knew what he ought to do but could not bring himself to it.

So, we do not see the Swiss baker at his best. Worn out, he climbs from bed at length and stands on the oilcloth, a pathetic figure in his long nightshirt, blear-eyed and dishevelled. Sadly he climbs into his working clothes, shaves and washes mechanically and descends to his afternoon meal.

"What's the matter, Axel?" asks his wife and his daughters make the same query with anxious eyes.

"I hafn't slept. It is nothing. Somehow my mind was occupied. The war... It will pass."

They know better than to press the matter further. Sometimes father is that way. When he's a bit off colour he gets an attack of *Sehnsucht*. Longing for home and thinking of his mother, after all these years. Of course, he used to go once a year in the good times. Now, he's quite cut off. Poor papa. He'll soon get over it. They leave him to his little sentimental mood, knowing it to be better that way.

Meister makes a show of eating one of his own meat pies copiously anointed with piccalilli. Then, he draws up a chair to the fire and his wife hands him his curved pipe and pouch. The girls bring matches and the daily paper. It is a ritual which Meister enjoys as a rule. Tonight, however, it hurts him. His eyelids begin to burn with what are suspiciously like suppressed tears. He tries to concentrate on the news which is bad and diverts him for a few minutes. Raising his eyes, he sees his cello, standing reproachfully in its corner. No more happy Thursday nights if...

"I'll be getting off to the bakery, I think," he says at length, thinking that immersion in his labours will bring relief.

"What, so early, dad?"

"Yes. It gets more and more tifficult nowadays. Changing the recipes to suit supplies, and trying to make things chust as before," he replies, with a sad smile and a gentle shrug of the shoulders.

In the familiar bakehouse, Mr Meister loses some of his worries. His job is a calling to him. He loves it. Even now, under difficult conditions, it is a challenge.

Bread, pies, pastry and the empty shells of other dainties. The master skilfully handles his limited quota of butter, sugar, dried eggs. Fairly to himself and fairly to the customers. Who can do more? His mind, concentrated on his task, forgets his troubles. Only now and then as he changes from one speciality to another, does the cloud float across his spirit. He shudders, shrugs in melancholy fashion and passes on. His wife joins him and together they finish the stuff for the ovens.

"You look tired out, Axel. Are you all right?"

"Yes, my dear. I'll be better after another sleep. I'm chust a bit jaded. The war and the weather... I'll get over it, and now you be off to bed."

She kisses him and leaves him to his labours by night. He loads the ovens with their first batch, carefully notes the time and sits for his first rest in a wooden armchair. Usually, he stays awake, thinking of the past and the present in the quiet hours when everyone else is asleep. Now, through a sleepless day, his head nods. A passing policeman tries the shop door and finds it fast. Meister is dreaming.

The Nankivell of the pastrycook's dream is a different figure from that of his waking hours. His uniform is more military; and does he wear an armlet with a hideous sign on his arm?

Meister stands before his desk, a diminutive figure, humble, aware of his guilt. The one-time kindly eyes of the Superintendent are now like steel and bore right into the baker's brain. Through the open door of the next room, Meister can see a quartet of musicians hard at it, soundlessly playing. The officer is speaking.

"Axel Adolf Meister, enemy of the State. Fifth columnist, impeding the ends of justice. Give me your permit. You will be deported to Dachau…"

All around stand the familiar members of the force, his friends. Not friends now, but harsh, military marionettes, ready to act at their chief's bidding. As at a cinema show, there pass before the victim's eyes the happy events of his life. Starting from scratch in England. Courting his wife. The birth of his daughters. The music. The friendly chatter of customers and fellow townsfolk in Swarebridge.

"But this is my home…"

"No longer your home. Traitor to the State."

Nankivell assumes such proportions and such a malevolent look that the terror of Meister wakes him. The little baker moans and opens his eyes. The familiar shelves, sacks, mixing-tables, troughs and boards, with the modern ovens towering in the background. He almost weeps and could embrace them all in his relief. Outside, a great hush pervades the place. A little black cat emerges from behind the flour bags and rubs round her master's trousers. Terror still holds him. All he has built up; all he loves is at stake! In the dim light, great shadows seem to wait to pounce on him. The little cat seems like a small patch of sanity in the horror of the night. Meister rises hastily, rushes into the shop, and dials Swarebridge 1111.

"Swarebridge police station," answers a terse voice, almost like those of his dream.

Mr Meister pours out his tale incoherently.

"Well, well, well," finally comes from the other end in a

changed, sane voice. "I'll tell Mr Nankivell first thing in the morning. Perhaps you'd care to call to see 'im about nine in the mornin'."

The baker's brain seems suddenly to click back into sanity. He feels a great load lifted from his spirit. Then a greater one descends.

"My bread! My bread! Mein Gott, my bread," he gasps and rushes back to his ovens chattering to himself. Somewhere a clock strikes twelve.

14

NIGHT PIECE

Axel Meister was not the only man to spend a disturbed night. As he walked home after his interview with Partington, Nankivell churned over the case in his mind. A murder in church seemed quite out of keeping with Doyle's character. In a pub. brawl or a street scene, perhaps yes; but in this case, most unlikely. Besides, what did the Irish cattle dealer know of the geography of Zion chapel, of The Famous Duke of York, of the trapdoor in the choir pew, or of the likelihood of Harbuttle's capering as he did? Furthermore, might not Doyle have bolted for some reason quite remote from the murder case — always assuming that he *had* bolted? No. Try again.

Nankivell's train of thought was interrupted by his arrival at his house. There he was obliged to thrust his musings into the background, for there was a domestic interlude of a minor but pleasant nature, hardly worth recording here. In a raffle, immediately instituted by some ladies of Zion after the withdrawal of the restraining hand of Harbuttle, the Superintendent's wife had won the first prize, a cake weighing several pounds. There was a carnival atmosphere about the place which Nankivell had not the heart to dispel by more brooding. He therefore took a liberal helping of the spoils and waited until his family had retired and the house was quiet. Then, with his pipe burning well and the dog convulsively dreaming beside him, he returned to his case.

First of all there was the motive.

The old chap had been quarrelsome and provocative, even to his own kith and kin. But it needs strong provocation to make anyone commit murder. If you're normal, you don't kill a man just because he happens to get on your nerves. On the other hand, someone overwrought, say Hewston or Partington, might perhaps turn nasty, very nasty, under stress. These two, however, had solid alibis. To start finding all the other people with kinks in Swarebridge was an impossible task.

Nankivell shuddered at his thoughts. If Zion nursed a cunning homicidal maniac, it was going to be a job! Before his mind's eye passed a procession of eccentric personalities, members of the congregation. Sin and vice hunters. Soul seekers and savers, intent on conversion of the erring or the utter destruction and damnation of the lost. Burning-eyed haters of all who broke the law and defied the prophets. Haggard or possessive spinsters, full of biting zeal for this or that man or cause or battling with all the mad strength of repression against lust and vice in others...

As though disturbed by the motley host conjured up by his master's brain, the dreaming setter at Nankivell's feet made nightmare running movements with his paws and yapped in dismal, muffled tones.

"All right, boy. All right," muttered the Superintendent, gently prodding the dog's ribs with a slippered toe. The animal opened one eye, yawned voluptuously and forthwith began to snore healthily.

Another motive, of course, might be the money. Singleton was known to be hard put to make ends meet. He'd no alibi and was the most likely candidate for the killer's title, except that he wasn't the right type. Anyone might kill in defence of home and family. And Harbuttle, by getting wed again, might deprive the Singletons and their offspring of their inheritance. Kill him before he could make a new will! It all fitted, except, of course, Singleton. A man without initiative, ambition, or guts. One who, when roused, became a flapping, spluttering, stammering stupid. Unlikely; but bear him in mind. The other possibilities, Harbuttle's housekeeper, Miss Sleaford, Mrs Singleton, even if they knew the contents of the old man's will, were physically incapable of murder of the type committed. That is granting they're sane...

The most likely reason was that Harbuttle had spotted some kind of hanky-panky going on during his frequent scrutiny of the view from Pisgah. That brought in Doyle again, among others. Suppose Doyle were the agent of the unseen one whom, according to Cuthbert Silversides, Harbuttle was browbeating on the fatal night. Perhaps some idol of Zion was about to be cast from his pedestal and struck blindly before it was too late. It was up to the police to lay Doyle by the heels, although it was going to be a difficult job. Even if the Irishman were traced, he could only be detained for questioning and, if he proved to be taking a perfectly legitimate holiday, he might be awkward to handle. If you *are* invested with police authority, you can't throw your weight about to the extent of dragging holiday-makers from the country or the seaside simply because they've left home rather hurriedly! Not in this country, at any rate. When Doyle was traced, it might be a hopeless task trying to get anything out of him. He might, with very good reason, say that the offal buried in his manure heap was from a cow which had died from natural causes. And the place apparently used as a slaughterhouse would then find its justification. The movements by night at his farm, too, might have a simple explanation. On the other hand, they might not. Better wait and see, but unless tactfully handled, this aspect of the case might result in a hell of a row.

Then, there was Butterfield and the hostilities about to break out between him and Harbuttle on the matter of the director-ship of Pogsley's. But Butterfield had an alibi. Why keep turning the thing over and over so persistently?

Burt, too, had his alibi. He had quarrelled with Harbuttle, but not mortally. Just one of the usual church squabbles, eventually patched up... Why were church people so touchy and crotchety? Not all of them, but those who were totally immersed in the place, spending all their time at it. Probably jealous for position and power...

Nankivell stretched himself and yawned. Better have his bottle of beer and get to bed. Not getting any nearer by turning the thing over and over, especially when he was tired after a long day. The Superintendent rose and the dog did likewise. They both yawned and stretched again in unison. Nankivell went to the pantry and took his bottle from a dark, cool corner. The dog eyed the meat safe and wagged his tail as though egging-on his master to mischief. Nankivell yielded to the appeal, found a chop bone and flung it to his companion. Together they returned to the dining room bearing their spoils. The man had just poured out his beer when the dog began to growl, softly and ominously. Then, he dropped his bone and barked belligerently. At a gesture from his master, the animal grew silent and returned to his bone. Shambling footsteps could be heard approaching along the road, halting now and then as if examining the houses or reading the names on the gates. The name of Nankivell's was *Mon Abri*. He hated it, but it wasn't his choice. Someone before him had had it put in the title deeds and he hadn't bothered to change it.

The footsteps paused at *Mon Abri*. The gate creaked. Clump, clump, scrunch...they resumed along the gravel path. Before the intruder could ring the bell or beat the knocker, Nankivell was there, the door open and his dimmed torch shining. He wasn't going to have his family and the whole neighbourhood disturbed at this hour of night, probably by some reveller off his course!

"Hullo, hullo, hullo," said a cheerful voice. "Ashked me to call, didn' yer? Found you out at poleesh station, so thought I'd find you at home. Ashked the landlord of Ring o' Bells where you lived... *Mon* something or other, he says, lookin' in the teleph... the telephone book. Only house with a French name in the road... So here I am. Got something to tell yer..."

It was Higgins from the searchlight camp. Evidently having a night off and made bold by liquor.

Nankivell was extremely annoyed and promised himself that once having quietly got rid of his newfound friend, he would take steps to see that he didn't call there again. Tomorrow, he'd have a word with the corporal-in-charge. He didn't mind hospitality, but at one in the morning and the recipient with a skinful already was too much!

"Evenin' Higgins. Late for you to be about. What's going to happen when you get back to camp? You'll be for it..."

"Oh, that's oright... Know how to get in without dishturbin' the boys. Trust your old Higgy..."

He guffawed loudly. Nankivell shuddered, thinking what his wife and the neighbours would say about his apparent roistering in the road in the small hours. Better give him a strong black coffee, sober him a bit, and send him on his way.

"Come in, Higgins, and be quiet about it. The rest of the family's in bed."

"Know 'ow to be quiet and dishcreet, sir," answered the visitor, stumbling into the hall and uncertainly following Nankivell into the sitting room. The sight of the Superintendent's bottled-beer, now gone flat and melancholy-looking in its glass, seemed to inspire Higgins.

"Ah, ahhhhh," he said in anticipation.

"No more for you, Higgins. Black coffee and then home to bed."

The dog growled disapproval of the newcomer and Nankivell took the animal with him into the kitchen, leaving Higgins breathing heavily and now grown shy and subdued as the light and atmosphere of the place began their sobering work. The soldier looked in bad shape. Evidently, he'd spent a night out with his cronies and had been over-treated.

Nankivell returned with the coffee, which Higgins began to sip gingerly and blow upon to cool it. In the end, he laid it down unsteadily.

"Called to tell you somethin'. Can't remember what it was, now," he said in a firmer voice. He ruminated owlishly.

"Ah, yesh."

He fumbled in his pocket and produced a copy of that day's *Swarebridge Sentinel*, the local organ published every Tuesday and Saturday. He struggled with the soiled sheets uncertainly, finally producing a picture of Alderman Harbuttle in mayoral robes and surrounded by a full account of his life and shameful death.

"That's the fellow at the house on the hill, eh? One who used ter watch the camp with his glasses? Landlord of the Ring o' Bells told me."

"That's right, Higgins. Why?"

"Well, you see, I never saw his face properly through the glasses when he was on the terrace of his house. Too far away, see? And invar...invari...well he allus had 'is glasses up to his face, see? His 'ouse was a good dishtance away, as well."

"Yes. Drink your coffee, Higgins..."

The soldier took a great gulp of the hot stuff and writhed as it burned its way down his gullet. It did him good and made him more collected and sheepish as the sobering work continued.

"Well, sir. One day I see that chap Harbuttle at the farm in the hollow."

"Toad-in-Hole?"

"The tumbledown place, yes. And he was talking hard to the chap that lives there."

"Doyle."

"That his name? Then they seemed to 'ave a proper row. I got interested, see? Thought I'd got a ringside seat for a scrap. But the old chap up and off and nothin' came of it."

"That's very interesting, Higgins. Why didn't you mention it before, when I saw you this morning?"

"I didn't know it was the same chap, guvnor. Then I see this paper at the pub, like, and remembered I'd bin talkin' to you about the same fellow. Well… I got treated to one or two more than I could stand. I seemed to remember that I'd got to see you and tell you. I orn't to 'ave come round like this and I'm sorry. I'll be goin' now and I'm 'opin' you'll overlook this."

"That's all right, Higgins. I'm glad you called and told me. Now have another cup of coffee, then get along as quietly as you can."

* * *

HIS VISITOR HAVING DEPARTED MORE STEADILY than he arrived and without, as Nankivell feared the most, having been sick on his wife's best carpet, the Superintendent locked up, cleared away the remnants of the party and turned the dog out at the back door. Smoking and leaning against the doorjamb waiting for the animal to return, the Superintendent felt much happier. Now, he'd something to get his teeth into once he got hold of Doyle…

As if in answer to a prayer, the telephone bell rang.

It was the man on night duty at the police station.

"'Ope I'm not disturbing you, sir. Doyle's been found at Holyhead. 'E was trying to get across to Dublin and got sore at being questioned about the h'exit formalities to Eire. So they told 'im he'd have to wait until tomorrer. The police there 'aving tipped the authorities the wink, like. Well, what does Doyle do, but get himself drunk and disorderly and gives the police there just what they want. They've run 'im in and got him there in custody. Will you ring 'em up tomorrer and arrange about goin' to see him?"

"Very good, sergeant. I'm glad they've got him. Now we can get on."

"Hope I didn't get you out o' bed, sir."

"No. I was up. Goodnight…"

"Oh, by the way, sir. I've 'ad Mr Meister, the baker, on. In a regular tear, 'e was. Wanted to speak to you and when I said you was out, he started to tell me 'is tale. I could 'ardly foller a word. He kept breakin' into German or somethin'. Sorry, I didn't get the 'ang of what he was saying. Somethin' about Saturday night at Zion and birds or somethin'…."

"Birds?"

"I think 'e must have had a couple and bin imaginin' things. Anyway, he's callin' round to see you in the mornin' about nine."

"Right, sergeant. Don't worry any more about it tonight. Goodnight."

Everything seemed to be happening at once and tomorrow things would perhaps begin to hum. Nankivell hoped so. He was tired of groping round in the dark.

"Whatever have you been doing?" said Mrs Nankivell, when at last her husband appeared in the bedroom. "Bells ringing, doors banging, feet tramping and voices about the place. From here, it sounded like the effects department of a dramatic society."

Nankivell grinned.

"Things are beginning to move, mother," he said.

15

TERROR TAKES MICHAEL DOYLE

During the weekend of the Zion anniversary, Michael Doyle had a jubilee of his own. He went off with a pal on Sunday morning and got gloriously drunk. It was a good thing that he had no stock to attend to on his miserable farm for, arriving home at two in the morning, thanks to that uncanny instinct which steers the boozer safely to port, he flung himself on his dirty, unmade bed, and slept the clock round with his boots on. He was in a weary state when he awoke. His curly, black hair was tousled, his clothes creased and soiled and he had lost the neckerchief which he always wore instead of a collar. His feet felt like swollen puddings in the heavy boots which he forthwith removed and padded round in his stockinged feet for relief.

Doyle looked at himself in the mirror and recoiled. His Irish blue eyes were bleary and ringed darkly. He hadn't shaved for three days and his small pointed nose was red from his debauch. In better days, he had been a handsome chap, with his crisp hair, laughing eyes, ruddy cheeks and his blarney. Many a girl had cast longing eyes at him, had her longings temporarily satisfied and then been left in the lurch. Now, thanks to personal neglect, excesses of all kinds, shady dealing and certain misgivings concerning some doubtful ventures he was mixed in, Doyle was bad-tempered, shifty and more unreliable than ever.

At any time, Doyle expected his landlord to give him notice to quit. The land he rented was in good heart, for he sub-let it to his neighbours, if such they might be called, but the house and buildings were disgracefully kept. Only two rooms of the small dwelling were in use. The bedroom we have inspected with Nankivell. The kitchen, with tiled floor and with a sink in one corner, held two wooden chairs and a rough table, the usual fitted cupboards and little else. When Doyle left the place on Sunday morning, the table was littered with dirty pots and scraps of food, the tiled floor was dirty and the whole place dusty and disordered. Clothing, rat and rabbit traps, a gun and cartridges, ropes, halters and a humane killer lay in corners here and there. The whole room stank of stale food, grease and decay, and the odour of the sink pervaded the air. The atmosphere was worse than ever when the owner came down-stairs after his drunken sleep, for added to the rest of the noisome smells was that of the piece of beef he had left on the table and which had gone bad. Large blue bottles buzzed about and frenziedly thrashed against the windows.

Doyle took a half-empty bottle of whisky from a corner cupboard, drank from it, swilled his mouth and throat raucously and spat in the sink. Then he took a longer draught and swallowed. Lighting an oil stove, he produced bacon and an egg or two and cooked himself a meal, stretching and yawning the while. The mess cooked, he decanted it from the dirty frying pan on to a plate and cut himself hunks of bread from a dry loaf. Ravenously the man devoured his meal, soaking his bread in the bacon fat, washing it down with whisky and water, shovelling the food into his mouth with spasmodic gestures, ruminating between the bites. Finally, he cleaned his plate with a piece of bread, sucked his fingers, and wiped his lips on the back of his hand. Rising, he pushed aside his dirty dishes and made for the sink, where he sluiced water over his head and face, drying himself on a ragged old towel. He fingered his cheeks and decided to shave. This operation he performed with an old-fashioned razor, an almost hairless brush and a piece of soap in an old coconut shell. He felt better for this titivating and went a step further to the extent of sorting out a new neckcloth from a jumble of articles in one of the drawers. Still in his stockinged feet, but looking more civilised, the Irishman took out a battered briar and charged it with tobacco, which he cut from a roll of twist. When this was going to his satisfaction, he began to look round for the daily paper. The latter he found behind the front door, where Lot Wilkins had pushed it via the letter slot. One of the simpleton's daily jobs was to call at the newsagents on his way to the farm. Doyle, his feet on the table, his pipe drawing noxiously, began to read. The clock whose striking mechanism had gone awry, made clicking noises indicating that it was about six o'clock. The daylight began to fade. Doyle turned the pages and read on.

SWAREBRIDGE MURDER.

ALDERMAN FOUND STABBED TO DEATH IN CHURCH.

POLICE BAFFLED.

HOMICIDAL MANIAC AT LARGE?

Doyle sprang to his feet like one stung. All his lethargy left him. He flung the newspaper to the floor and stared wildly around with unseeing eyes. A great fear gripped him. Hastily he poured out a cupful of neat whisky and gulped it down. Then he felt better and stood thinking for a while.

"Holy Mother!" he said to himself. "He's done him in."

In his prime Doyle had been a fine, strong fellow. His stocky, well-built frame was still evidence of this. He was good for a fight at any time, especially of the concerted, catch-as-catch-can type, in which many are involved, and half-bricks are not barred. On odd occasions, he might engage in single combat, but this form of warfare did not appeal to him, being too exacting. He had a streak of cowardice in him which always kept an eye on the line of retreat or sought safety in numbers. Against the unseen, Doyle was no use at all. His Celtic imagination worked hard against him, wore down his nerves and resistance.

The news before him started Doyle's imagination going like a dynamo. Slowly, with gathering momentum, heightened tension and terrifying power.

Only on Saturday morning last the murdered man had been round at Toad-in-Hole, snooping about, asking questions. Doyle had told him to go to hell and mind his own business. Whereat Harbuttle, as he was called, had told Doyle that hell was the place where he, Doyle, was bound for. He had also said that he knew of the racket that was going on and intended to put a stop to it...

Harbuttle had mentioned the name of the boss, and he must have faced him with the business. So the boss had shut his mouth for him.

Beads of sweat almost as large as peas burst out on the Irishman's forehead. He had no taste for being the next victim, which was quite likely. After all, he and Lot Wilkins were the only two who were really in the game. Lot didn't understand what it was all about. A harmless loony. But the boss might decide, now that he'd a killing to add to his other crimes, that Doyle's silence was the next thing.

Doyle whimpered as his imagination stung him and ran away with his common sense. Hastily he put on his boots and laced them with trembling fingers. He took up one of the tiles of the dirty floor and from the hollow beneath it drew a wad of notes. These he stuffed in his pocket. The only emotion his fear generated was flight. He was off out of all this!

Upstairs, the fugitive opened drawers and hurled clothing

into a fibre suitcase. He didn't know what to take and what to reject of the welter of personal odds and ends, but instinctively packed his belongings whilst turning over his plans in his mind in dazed fashion. His one aim was to put Swarebridge and Toad-in-Hole behind him as quickly as possible. Now and then, in the course of his preparations for flight, the man paused and listened, as if anticipating the arrival of what he feared at any moment. At length, after two or three false alarms, he settled down in earnest to fasten his bag. The catch was broken on one side and he sought stout cord to bind round it. He was preoccupied in his search when, suddenly, the event he feared happened. There was a loud banging on the backdoor, which gave access to the farmhouse from the yard.

Doyle almost screamed with fright at this sudden alarm. Instinctively he brought his hand down on the candle and extinguished it.

More knocking.

"Come on, Doyle, let me in," roared a voice, the one he had expected, from below. The thumping on the door was repeated. "Hi, Doyle. Come down. I know you're in, man. Let me in."

The Irishman held his breath and gazed round in fear, trying to pierce the gloom and endeavouring to set his racing thoughts in order and think what next to do. He again removed his boots and softly crept downstairs. Raincoat and cloth cap from the passage. These he put on breathlessly. He could hear his visitor grumbling to himself and snorting outside. Then, kicking at the door again.

Upstairs sped the terrified man, his fears magnified tenfold by the darkness and uncertainty. He felt his limbs almost refusing to obey his will, like a nightmare. As he brought the suitcase down, an ominous quiet pervaded. The fugitive stood like a statue, listening, trying to pick up the slightest vestige of sound. At length, footsteps were heard going into the farmyard. Doyle gently sobbed with relief, but not for long, for he heard his visitor scuffling with the ladder which lay along the wall. He heard it placed against the side of the house.

"Come on, Doyle, or I'm coming up for you. I've seen the light, so be showing yourself."

Silence.

Heavy footsteps mounted the ladder. Doyle, his heart beating like a sledgehammer, softly opened the front door and let himself out. Thence, an overgrown path led through fields to the main road. Still in his stockinged feet and carrying his boots and case, the fleeing man broke into an unsteady run, lurching over the sharp pebbles of the track, not feeling the pain in his terror. Across two fields and over two stiles. The man paused. Hearing no sound, he bent and put on his boots, his fingers stiff and almost refusing to function. Then he was off again, running for dear life until he struck the main road. He did not slacken his pace until he reached the station. In ten minutes, the train to Whitemore Junction was due. Doyle felt no relief until he was safely in a dark compartment. At last, he relaxed and slumped down with fatigue, too exhausted to take any interest in the journey, only aware that he was safe and that the wheels were beating a steady rub-a-dub-dub. The last train had gone when he reached Whitemore and he spent the night in the station waiting room.

After changing twice and travelling by slow train, Doyle reached Holyhead the following night. The place was as black as pitch and a sea mist was drifting over the harbour. The cross-channel packet was tied-up at the dock, with here and there a very dim light showing. Travellers moved about in the darkness, like shades eager to be ferried over the Styx. Doyle booked his ticket to Eire and ate a sandwich and washed it down with whisky at the buffet. He felt a bit better. He was full of fears and misgivings still.

Suppose they thought he'd killed Harbuttle and chased him. After all, the old blighter had probably been seen when kicking up his row at Toad-in-Hole last Saturday. But Doyle had an alibi. The murder in the church was committed whilst he was drinking at The Old Duke and there were plenty there to bear out his tale. No. What gave speed to Doyle's heels was the fact that the boss had started killing to keep himself clear. If he didn't hesitate at a man like Alderman Harbuttle, small fry like Doyle wouldn't count. The Irishman bought and swallowed another double whisky. He prepared to face the customs and exit officers. As he made his way to the sheds, a thought struck him. Suppose the Swarebridge police had sent out a call for him to the ports! Better not give the name of Doyle... Mulcrone, his mother's name. That would do. In his haste he forgot something.

"Name?" said the official.

"Mulcrone," said Doyle, boldly and with his best brogue.

"Nationality?"

"Irish Free State..." Quite true.

"Papers."

Doyle halted. His identity card and letters were in the name of Michael Doyle. Fool!

"They're in me suitcase at the office. I'll be gettin' them," said Doyle, and left the shed and made for the open air to think out his problem. Damn. He'd have to wait, declare his true name, taking the risk, and hope for a different officer next time. Hopeless to try for this boat now. Better find a room in the town and wait until the next. After enquiring the next sailing, he made for the refreshment room again. Another double whisky to clear his brain and buck him up.

Meanwhile, the exit officer had given the nod to a man in plain clothes.

The girl at the bar refused to serve Doyle with another drop. Whisky was scarce and he'd had more than his ration. Doyle flared up in wrath. His emotions of the last thirty hours turned to annoyance. He gave the length of his tongue to the waitress.

So much so, that another Irishman, standing nearby, intervened. Doyle grew noisy, shouting louder, threatening to have the skin off the champion of the girl. This was the chance of the man who had been watching Doyle.

"Now you," he said. "That's enough. Causing a disturbance, eh?"

Doyle's language grew more lurid. The big newcomer seized his collar in a grip of iron.

"Now you'll come with me. Drunk and disorderly."

So Doyle got another free night's lodging.

16

DOYLE TALKS

Doyle spent the night abusing the police and loudly calling for the Irish "ambassador." The former were not disturbed but greatly amused by the request for the latter. Finally, tired out, the prisoner lapsed into a stupor and at length fell asleep. It was dawn when he awoke. Thanks to his vocal efforts of the night before, he was hoarse and could heap no further vituperations on the head of the cheerful constable who gave him his breakfast. Meanwhile, Nankivell had sworn out a warrant for the arrest of Doyle on a charge of keeping an illegal slaughterhouse and evading justice by flight, and Patchett took the police car and the most phlegmatic constable in the Swarebridge force and set out for Holyhead at dawn to bring the wanderer home. The police at the port arranged for their prisoner to be released with a caution, whereupon, to his intense disgust, he was seized upon by Patchett and partner on another charge.

"What the hell…" yelled Doyle as the warrant was read to him. "Give me my solicitor or the consul for Eire before I do somebody bodily harm."

"Now, Doyle, just behave yourself and come along quietly.

We've a lot to talk to you about and if you act like a sensible man, it will go better with you," suggested Patchett in his cheerful voice and this seemed to aggravate the accused the more.

"Oi will assist the police of no foreign potentate," he announced loudly and with an effort at dignity, endeavouring to assert his Irish nationality, which suddenly seemed to have grown dear to him.

"All the same, Doyle, you're coming back to Swarebridge with us," was the reply.

The Irishman's mottled complexion turned chalky white.

"Never," he said and squared-up as if to fight.

"Yes," said Patchett, pulling himself up to his full height, whereupon Doyle collapsed like a burst balloon.

"I prefer to answer the charge here, which I will do, decent and respectful," he replied, now grown mild and with a trace of pleading in his tone.

"I'm afraid that's impossible, Doyle. You'll have to come back with us."

"But, I can't…"

"No such thing as can't, Doyle. Now be movin'."

"Will I be in custody all the time…? I don't want bail, then."

"Nobody's going to force bail on you, always granting that it's allowable."

"If you'll be responsible for my safety, then I'll come quiet. Otherwise, I'll resist."

"In that case, we'll have to handcuff you. But you'll be all right with us."

Reluctantly Doyle followed.

On the way to Swarebridge Doyle had the company of PC Eaves, an officer who never knew what to say next. The pair of them occupied the back seat, with Patchett driving in front. Doyle, therefore, had time to let his imagination run riot on the reason for his arrest. Illegal slaughterhouse be damned, he thought. They're tempting me back to pin murder on me. Whereupon he began to question his companion, who remained mute and evinced no annoyance whatever at his prisoner's language, but took out a pair of handcuffs, jingled them ominously and smiled as Doyle relapsed into moodiness again.

At the end of the journey, Nankivell took the Irishman in hand at once.

"Well, Doyle, so you're back, I see."

"Yes, and somebody will be made to sit up for this day's work when I see my solicitor," replied Doyle.

"The charge you've been brought back on is a minor one, Doyle. The main one's murder…"

The prisoner's truculence left him. He had no stomach for this business. His imagination had already played ducks and drakes with his nerves and his staying powers were almost gone.

"You've got nothin' on me for that. I never see Harbuttle after he left me last Saturday morning."

"How do you know it's Harbuttle we're thinking of? There's been another murder since. A youngster this time…"

Doyle's only answer was a hoarse cry.

"Yes. A nasty business. Unpleasant being even an accessory to murder, Doyle. So talk, if you value your reputation."

"I've nothing to do with murderin' anybody, and I know nothin' about it."

"You were seen quarrelling with the old chap on Saturday morning, you know."

"But I've an alibi for when he was killed. I was at The Old Duke all Saturday night. Lots will tell you, I never left until after eleven and was there by seven, or just after. Logan, the landlord, Dan Harris, the barman, Fenney and Marshlade…they'll all put in a word for me. You can't get me for that."

"But where were you Monday night when the other murder was committed?"

"What other?"

"The little lad. Nobody says the two are connected…"

"But what should I be doin' killin' little boys? I like children. They're all dear to me heart, bless 'em."

"Cut that out. We're getting nowhere. Now, Doyle, you've been running an illegal slaughterhouse, haven't you?"

"You've no proof of that. You're guessing…"

"Very well. Suppose we are guessing. The proofs will be here very shortly when the men I've sent to turn your rubbish heap over and question a dozen or so butchers hereabouts, come back. Meanwhile, you can go free, but don't leave the town, Doyle."

The Irishman began to hedge and stammer.

"I don't want to go free. I'll wait here until you prove what you've got against me. I'll wait…"

"Why so eager, Doyle? We don't want your company here. Let him go, Patchett. He'll not bolt a second time."

"Come on, Doyle, off you go," said Patchett, taking the Irishman by the shoulder and making for the door.

"I don't want to go. What did you bring me here for, if it's only to let me go? It's not safe for me here, I tell you…"

The man's nerve had broken, and he was scared to death.

"Not safe!" said Nankivell. "Why, what's a brave lad like you afraid of? Come now, off you go."

"I want police protection again' somebody. He was after me on Monday night… He'll be after me again if he knows I'm about."

"Suppose you tell us who this giant is that scares the terrible Doyle, the terror of the police and afraid of no man. That's what you said once, isn't it, when you were hauled in drunk?"

"I can't tell you… I can't. He'll…he'll kill *me* next."

Doyle's face was green with terror.

"Show him the door, Patchett."

"All right, all right. I'll talk. But I won't go out of this place. Keep me in the cells, deport me, do anything you like, but..."

"Sit down. Give him a glass of water...yes, water, Patchett."

Doyle drank with a grimace.

"Now, Doyle."

"Well, I *have* been runnin' a slaughterhouse on the quiet. I'll confess. Black market meat sells well, and I was tempted. I'll stand my trial and take my punishment."

"Who's behind all this?"

"What do you mean?"

"You're not running this racket yourself. Who did Harbuttle say he was going to see when he left you? Now come on, Doyle, no more of this..."

"We used to slaughter the cattle at my place and cut the carcasses and distribute them. Long distances we went. Took them in my vans. Some are always ready to pay good prices for a bit of extra, like. Eggs, too, we used to collect and distribute the same."

"Yes, Doyle. You bought and collected the cattle and then distributed it when it was meat; but who found the money? You were busy, Doyle, doing an extensive business, weren't you? You hadn't money to pay the cash down needed for that kind of trade. You're no expert at slaughtering, to say nothing of cutting up the carcasses, are you? Who was your partner? Harbuttle was murdered because he found out what you were at. He told you he'd found out, didn't he, last Saturday? He spotted something going on through field-glasses from his house and then, one night, he saw something even stranger going on when the men at the searchlight illuminated your little activities by having a practice with their light just in the middle of your manoeuvres. Harbuttle watched you after that. He was pretty near you a night or two and saw both you and your pals at work. One of your gang was quite a big shot. So big, that Harbuttle wanted the joy of unmasking him publicly and bringing about his downfall. That's why he was killed."

"How do you know all this? Sounds like a made-up tale to me."

"I can substantiate every word, Doyle. Harbuttle's house-keeper tells me he spent a late night or two prowling. We know where, and so do you. Now you're an accessory in this case and you can choose the way you're going. Trial for murder or help the police. No more delay. Out with it..."

Doyle had gone grey-cheeked with fear. He licked his dry lips and looked around him with bloodshot eyes.

"Right. But if I tell, I get a fair deal. This will prove I hadn't any part in murderin' anybody. All I've done is truck in meat. That's all. The man who found the money was Burt. He found the customers for the secret meat, he found the money for the cattle, and he prepared it for delivery after slaughter. Harbuttle, when he came to my place on Saturday morning, said he'd seen Burt the night before and knew what he was at down at my place. He'd expose the whole thing, he said. I went up to tell Burt, but he was out and I daren't leave a message. So I got drunk. I thought the old man was just fooling. Never thought he had proof. How could he have had...? He'd *seen* us. But it was his word against Burt's wasn't it?"

"Go on. Why did you run out on Monday?"

"I didn't get home until nearly dark. Then I see in the paper that Harbuttle's been done in. I know who's done it. I also know that whoever's done it knows that I know. I got scared. Specially when I heard him round the place shouting for me. I nipped out of another door and made off as fast as me legs would carry me..."

"It was Burt?"

"Yes..."

"You don't happen to know, Doyle, do you, that Burt has a

perfectly good alibi? He was at Moggridge's farm at the time of the crime."

"What! So he didn't do it, after all. And here have I been talking all this time and scared to death that he'd do me in for knowing him to be a murderer. I withdraw what I've said. It was made under threats and compulsion."

"You'll be kept in the cells until the police court sits and then you'll be charged with illegal marketing and slaughtering. Take him away, Eaves."

"I demand bail... I want my solicitor," yelled the prisoner hoarsely, and was borne off to the lock-up.

Nankivell scratched his head and blew out his cheeks.

"What do you think of that, Patchett?"

"He's not lying, sir. But neither was Moggridge when I spoke to him about Burt's alibi. Moggridge is one of the straightest men hereabouts. Word's always as good as his bond and the local cattlemen and farmers would trust him with their lives. Very religious, is Moggy. Belongs to a special sect of very pious folk and practises what he preaches."

"Well, it's quite evident that Burt was in at the illegal meat racket. You know what that means. Perhaps a few thousands of a fine and two or three years in jail. That wouldn't suit our Councillor Burt. He's hot-tempered, too. Might easily have done-in Harbuttle in a fit of rage. But there's the alibi to get over. Mind if I go over your ground and call on Moggridge myself later? I don't know the chap at all, and I'd like to see what he's like."

"I don't mind a bit, sir. You'll find him very decent and probably you'll agree with me about his probity."

"No doubt I will. Now we've another visitor. Mr Meister's due any time. Should have been in at nine this morning, but I had to put him off through this Doyle business. He's a tale to tell about something he saw on Saturday night. There he is, I think."

Talk of the devil! It was the baker himself and he was suitably dressed for the ceremonial occasion. All in sober black, with a white winged collar, cravat and tiepin. His moustache was pomaded, and his glasses sparkled from much polishing. Only his eyes bore traces of uneasiness. He looked hesitantly from one officer to the other. The police were his friends, but last night's dream... Gott! He hadn't been able to get it out of his mind. Suppose they took offence at his remaining silent so long...

"Good afternoon, Mr Meister. Good of you to call," said Nankivell, and shook the little Swiss man by the hand. Patchett courteously followed suit. Very polite these foreigners. Better return the compliment. Can't let the force down. Although when they raise their hats to you in the street, well...it's a bit embarrassing. However... Patchett's musings were broken by a burst of shouting from Doyle, who was calling for his lawyer again. Meister looked startled.

"It's all right, Mr Meister. Only a disorderly prisoner. Nobody's harming him. He's just abusing us a bit," said Nankivell with a smile, and he offered his visitor his tobacco pouch. Meister accepted with a bow, took a seat and produced a large pipe with a porcelain bowl and a complicated sluice arrangement for keeping the tobacco dry. Patchett restrained a grin with difficulty, as he watched his chief's stock vanish into the capacious reservoir.

Meister's eyes shone and he twisted his moustache with modest pride. He was a friend of the police and was proud of it. For the first time since his horrible dream, he felt comforted and he smiled happily.

Then he remembered the purpose of his call on the police and thinking of his quintet, he grew sad again.

17

WHAT MEISTER SAW

"Now, Mr Meister, and what can we do for you?" said Nankivell when the Swiss pastry cook had settled himself and his large pipe.

"I hope I hafen't been guilty of misdemeanour in not coming to you before, Superintendent," replied Meister looking questioningly at Nankivell, "But I was not aware until late yesterday that you were seeking information about what might haf happened at Zion Church last Saturday. I was there and in the kitchen round about the time of the unfortunate murder. I gather you are wanting news about who was thereabouts at that time?"

"Yes. Thanks for coming round."

"Not at all. As you know, I was doing the catering and about eight-thirty called to gather up the trays and other things which usually accompany cakes and such like things."

Meister spoke good English with precision and only now and then a trace of foreign accent.

"Yes, Mr Meister, and you saw someone?"

"I saw the back of someone, but I knew who it was. It was Mr Burt, the butcher!"

"Ah! Did he see you?"

"No. He went through one door as I entered by the other."

"But you're sure it was him?"

"I am quite sure it was he."

Nankivell smiled and stood corrected.

"Any idea what he was doing there?"

"No, Superintendent. But he seemed in a hurry to get out. He must haf heard me approaching and not wished to be seen there at that time."

"Yes. And did anything else happen?"

"No, except a liddle boy put in his head, apparently thinking nobody was there, but seeing me, ran off."

"Dear me. That would be poor Willie, the lad who was killed. So he didn't see the murderer there after all, but through talking in his presence about being in the kitchen, he was silenced."

Meister looked relieved at getting his story off his chest and rose to go.

"There's nothing more to tell, Superintendent. So, I will go, eh?"

"Yes. Thanks very much for your help, Mr Meister. You have assisted us a lot. I'll get you to sign a statement later."

"A pleasure, sir, a great pleasure," said the smiling visitor and with his pipe going merrily, he departed a happy man.

Nankivell now became very active.

"Put a man on Burt's track right away, and don't let him out of our sight until we've cleared up this business one way or another. We can't arrest him until Moggridge's alibi has been tested again. I can't understand it at all. Doyle and Meister have just independently incriminated Burt. Yet, according to Moggridge, he was at his farm at the time of the crime. There was no misunderstanding of the question as you put it to him the other day, was there, Patchett?"

"No. I put a straight question and got a straight answer. I

155

even refrained from mentioning the time, sir, and Moggridge gave that."

"I'd better be off to his farm, then."

"I've been thinking, sir," said Patchett. "Could the knife possibly have been fixed to something in the floor and have impaled Harbuttle, so to speak, when he fell down the trap?"

"I had that in mind but dismissed it. Nobody falling on a knife could possibly have got a wound like that. It was an expert's blow delivered with precision. Not one booby-trap in ten million would do such a job. Everything now points to Burt, except that confounded alibi sweeps the board."

"In what particular way, sir?"

"First, motive. Burt was apparently faced with exposure, imprisonment and disgrace if Harbuttle informed the police of his illicit slaughtering of cattle and trade in meat. We can only assume that Burt was the one whom the old man buttonholed in the classroom and gave a chance to confess to us, or else Harbuttle threatened to tell us himself. That's the tale as told by young Cuthbert Silversides and I see no reason for doubting it under the circumstances, do you?"

"No. Seems quite in keeping with the rest, sir."

"We know Burt to be a hot-tempered, impulsive chap. We also know that he was present at the argument at the Constitutional Club, when Harbuttle made his ridiculous boast that he'd beat the bounds of the place, upstairs and down, at Zion Chapel, with his follow-my-leader game."

"Silly fool...!"

"Yes. An utter ass, with no sense of humour and dominated by a senile desire to show off, I guess. It's well known that I call for my wife after these affairs at Zion. Harbuttle seems to have given Burt until my arrival as a sort of grace. If Burt himself cared to disclose the whole affair and his hand in the illicit dealing, the alderman would be satisfied; otherwise, Harbuttle would tell me himself."

"A self-righteous, schoolmasterish way of dealing, I think."

"Quite. But you see, Harbuttle and Burt were on the Town Council together. Burt's a forceful, headstrong type and many a time has stood up to the alderman. Harbuttle never forgot a grievance. Take the case of his organising resistance to Tilly Burt's application as organist of Zion. Harbuttle's no musician. Doesn't know a B from a bull's foot in music. Yet, for sheer cussedness and perhaps mean revenge, he got the girl turned down..."

"Yes."

"Well, let's assume that Harbuttle delivered his ultimatum to Burt and left it at that. The butcher grows more furious the more he thinks about it. Whilst all the bustle of the tea party and the clearing up afterwards is taking place, he can't do anything, but having made up his mind that nothing short of the death of Harbuttle can save him, Burt decides to kill him. If he'd gone home and slept on it, his fury might have died down, but he couldn't do that because Harbuttle's ultimatum expired just after my arrival. Then the lights of the main hall were lowered for the entertainment. Perhaps Burt thought he'd manage to silence his torturer in the dark, but there were others prowling round. Old people leaving early and parents gathering up their children and pottering off home. When *they'd* got away, Harbuttle himself got busy, proposing to Muriel Arrowsmith! Burt couldn't get him alone and you can well imagine his state of mind as the time ticked away."

"Then, someone played right into Burt's hands, by saying that it was time that Harbuttle began his Famous Duke of York! It all came back to Burt. Upstairs and downstairs in the chapel the old fool had said. Even if he'd repented, which was unlikely for a man of the alderman's mentality, no harm would be done by throwing open the trapdoor in the gallery. If he persisted, however, he'd fall right into the murderer's lap, so to speak. The black-out forced darkness upon them, added to the fact that leading his troupe into the dark was a part of the general scheme of excitement every year. Also, if the one following the alderman in the file fell down with him, in the melee, Burt could distinguish his victim and do the trick just the same."

"You might almost say that Harbuttle asked to be killed, in a manner of speaking, sir."

"Quite right. In Burt we have motive, opportunity, and also the temperament of the killer. Hot-temper, impulsiveness, and strength. The very man for delivering a blow such as despatched Harbuttle. Who could be more expert and thorough at the job than a butcher?"

"Looks as if we've got our man there, sir," said Patchett, carried away by enthusiasm at Nankivell's narrative.

"Except that he had an alibi, Patchett; except that he wasn't there at all when the crime was committed, and a witness of repute had testified that Burt was with *him*. So there we are. I ought to be with Moggridge, instead of talking here. I'm off, then. By the way, what about the man to keep an eye on Burt?"

"There's a plainclothes man watching Burt's back entrance from the loft of the livery stable behind, and the man on point duty in High Street is keeping an eye on the front door. I thought it would be less conspicuous and suspicious that way, sir."

"When did you give instructions? You haven't left the room since I told you."

"I thought we'd better do it after our talk with Doyle, so I gave the necessary orders then."

"Good man. I don't know what I'd do without you, Patchett." Patchett blushed.

1 8

THE HOLY OCCUPIER

Benjamin Moggridge was the fourteenth child of his father, who founded a new sect and made a church for them in a disused barn. Elihu Moggridge, the aforesaid patriarch, now gathered to his fathers for thirty years or more, was, in his prime, a convert to Mormonism. He would probably have gone the whole hog and emigrated to Salt Lake City but for two obstacles. One: his family had owned Leather Lea Farm and its two hundred and fifty fertile acres for six generations before him and it was in his blood, beloved and profitable. Two: he was married to a very masterful partner whose possessiveness and iron will precluded anything in the way of Mormon polygamy. So Old Elihu had to be content with founding a branch of Latter Day Saints himself, with one or two doctrinal alterations to make it fit in with his own and the views of Mrs Moggridge, mainly the latter. He called his followers The Holy Occupiers. They worshipped in the renovated barn and dipped their converts in a reservoir specially created and filled for ceremonial occasions by damming the stream. Mrs Moggridge compensated for the connubial restrictions by herself raising offspring to her husband to the tune of eight daughters and six sons. Benjamin was the lastborn, as his name implied, and was left in full possession of the farm and the Occupiers, his parents ceasing to occupy long after two girls and three boys had died in infancy, six of the daughters had married and scattered themselves and their issue elsewhere like the sands of the seashore, and two sons had migrated to Salt Lake City, there to follow the parent sect to the full.

Old Ben, at the age of eighty, was still going strong. He and his wife provided the bulk of the Occupiers' congregation themselves, for they had five sons and six daughters and a flock of grandchildren. Five others, very old people from round about, joined the family at worship. One and all were simple, bigoted and stubbornly faithful to the letter of the creed, which the late Elihu said was revealed to him, lock stock and barrel, in a dream.

Leather Lea was over two miles from Swarebridge in the heart of beautiful country. Law and order was under the care of a village constable, Lugg, who lived at Brinscombe, but who was under Nankivell's jurisdiction. The Superintendent had no qualms, therefore, in poaching on Lugg's preserves and made for Moggridge's on his bicycle. There he found Ben and his eldest son, Bazaleel, a youngster of sixty, cleaning out the dipping-pool, for on the approaching Sabbath, Bazaleel's Benjamin, aged eighteen, was to be received into full membership of the Occupiers by being thrice immersed.

Moggridge the elder was a rare old fellow. Six feet tall, bony, and with hardly a bend in his back, he had a fine head of thin, white hair and a magnificent grey spade beard which reached to his chest. His hands were large, long and knotted, his eyes stern steely blue, with a pale line round the iris of each which gave him the appearance of seeing right through anything. His son was an emasculated replica of his sire, for his back was twisted as if by severe cricks, his pate was almost bald, and his beard was thin and stringy. Both were stooping over the pool when

Nankivell arrived. The father straightened himself with a jerk and the son followed suit by painful degrees.

"Good afternoon, gentlemen," said Nankivell wheeling up his bike.

"Good day, friend, God bless you," said Ben without the least trace of sanctimoniousness.

"…day…bless you," muttered his son, who was like a shadow of his parent and completely under his domination.

"I've called to have a word with you about Mr Burt's visit here last Saturday, Mr Moggridge. Do you mind confirming the time he was with you? Eight-thirty to nine-thirty, I believe."

"That is right, brother. I've already said as much to your other colleague. What more do you want of me?"

"You are quite sure of those times?"

Ben Moggridge fixed Nankivell sternly with his ancient steely eye.

"The truth is a part of my creed and I do not depart from it. I neither swear on oath nor tell a lie, but my word is my bond. I have said it."

"He has said it," muttered the filial echo.

Nankivell was at a loss. Obviously, the old fellow would not stand for an inquisition, yet everything but Burt's alibi pointed to who had murdered Harbuttle.

"You must forgive my apparently doubting your word, Mr Moggridge, but your testimony is of great importance. We have, as you know, the murder of Mr Harbuttle and a little boy on our hands and are testing every statement about anyone likely to be concerned."

"Yes, friend, and rightly so, although man's vengeance for the shedding of his brother's blood is poor and uncalled for. Vengeance is mine, saith the Lord, I will repay."

"Yes. But there's a law of the land to which we must all subscribe, Mr Moggridge. We can't be our own law, whatever we believe. The machinery is set up by the majority, sir, and is for the best. We can't have murderers running about in the countryside, can we?"

"Ah, you haven't seen the light, friend. I can see that. Many are called, but few chosen," said the patriarch benignly. "However, we'll leave it at that, friend. I don't believe in conversion except by the spirit, which bloweth where it listeth. I have spoken."

The last phrase was uttered without arrogance and Nankivell took it that the old man was pronouncing some form of Amen to terminate the interview.

The Superintendent felt chagrined. He had drawn a blank and might well have expected it. Moggridge's reputation in the neighbourhood for straight dealing and probity was of the highest. There was nothing else for it but to withdraw as gracefully as possible.

"I must be getting back then," said Nankivell. "Please don't think I doubted your story in the first place, but in a serious matter of this kind, we can't be too sure."

"Say no more about it, brother…"

Old Moggridge took out a large and ancient silver watch and consulted it gravely. His son looked anxiously at him.

"That's another job well done, Bazaleel, all ready for the Lord's Day now. I think we'd better get away and see how the milking's doing. The day is hot for the time of year…"

Nankivell turned his bike heading for home and was about to bid the two farmers good day.

"… Will you take a glass of milk with me, Mr Nankivell?"

Nankivell was on the point of politely declining. Then, he paused. No use accepting defeat like this. He'd try again.

Old Moggridge looked at him invitingly. Hospitality to the stranger was one of his firmest beliefs, but he never asked anyone twice.

Also, the sect was strictly teetotal.

"Thanks. I don't mind if I do," replied the Superintendent, more from expediency than thirst.

They passed the meeting house on their way indoors. A small, whitewashed place through the open door of which Nankivell could see plain wood forms and a small, bare pulpit with a bible open on the reading desk. On the outer wall was a notice board.

CHURCH OF THE HOLY OCCUPIERS.
MEETINGS FOR WORSHIP
EACH LORD'S DAY
AT 10.30 MORNING
AND 6.30 EVENING.
GOD'S TIME AND GOD WILLING.
"OCCUPY TILL I COME."

"God's Time" had been added after the rest and was crushed in, and out of line. Nankivell just noticed it in passing and almost ignored it, but as they crossed the neat farmyard to the dairy, the truth came to him in a flash. He could hardly wait to confirm his conclusion. Old Moggridge produced two glasses of milk. His son seemed to have vanished about other business.

"Here's to your very good health, sir," said the police officer.

"God be praised for his bounty," replied the other, and they drank. Nankivell looked at his watch. A minute to four. He waited with growing excitement. Outside, milking was in progress. Churns and buckets rattled, feet clattered across the cobblestones, and the men and girls came and went with the milk.

The dairy door was open and beyond lay the kitchen. Almost before he was aware of what had happened, the clock in the room beyond struck the hour in rapid ringing strokes. Three! As if to confirm it, a mighty-sounding timepiece somewhere in the heart of the farmhouse broke into solemn chimes and told the hour with deep gravity. Three!!

"Your clocks are an hour late, Mr Moggridge," said Nankivell with as much unconcern as he could muster.

"No, my friend, they're *right*. You're wrong. Me and my house go by God's time, not man's."

Nankivell sensed faulty logic somewhere, but he was no metaphysician.

"You mean, you don't put the clock on for Summer Time?"

"The sun in the heavens tells the hour of noon. That is God's time and far be it from me to make it otherwise. It served our fathers well in days past and it shall be mine, too."

With a feeling of inward merriment Nankivell noticed that the men and maids at milking were scuttering around, however, to be in time for the dairy lorries which collected the churns by Summer Time schedule!

"So, that although Mr Burt was here from eight-thirty to nine-thirty last Saturday..."

"Yes, he called to say that he was thinking of taking a small farm himself and wished to bespeak some of my prize cattle if I'd sell..."

"...although he was here from eight-thirty to nine-thirty by your clocks, he was by Summer Time with you between nine-thirty and ten-thirty?"

"If you will have it so, yes, friend. But why call it Summer Time? Devil's time, I call it. Confusing man and his works and even upsetting the beasts of the field. God's time for me, may His name be praised!"

"You'd have saved us a lot of trouble if you'd made the true time plain to my colleague when he met you in the market, Mr Moggridge."

"Why should I? I don't recognise this devil's time, nor do any of my family. We work to the old, true time, as shown by the sun, heaven's clock. If your man had asked me in terms of the time I recognise, there would have been no trouble or confusion."

Nankivell could see that it was no use arguing. Burt had known where to seek an alibi and had trusted to luck and old Moggridge's eccentricity to get him through. The finger had been laid on Burt purely through accident, but he had kept this alibi up his sleeve in case of need. He had trumped-up an excuse for visiting the old Occupier, after killing Harbuttle, rushing from the chapel in the hubbub and using his car, which could easily cover the distance in a quarter of an hour. In the black-out and in the room darkened for the entertainment, nobody would notice the comings and goings, especially as Burt had made a point of only being partially restored to the fold of Zion after his quarrel with the powers-that-be of the Church.

Nankivell bade a friendly goodbye to old Benjamin, who gave him his parting blessing without hesitation or invitation.

As the Superintendent pedalled into the main road, he saw the familiar, portly bulk of PC Lugg approaching in full sail towards him. He dismounted for a word with his subordinate.

"Good arternoon, sir," said Lugg, with a friendly smile from ear to ear. "Bin wisitin' the Moggridges, I see."

"Yes. Just a bit of routine business with the old man, Lugg. How are you and the family?"

"Oh, fine. All of us. Rum old codger Moggridge, ain't he?"

"Yes. Some cranky ideas with that religion of his."

"Not 'arf. Gives us quite a bit o' trouble now and then, sir. I 'ad no end o' bother with 'im about the black-out at fust. Couldn't make 'im see sense and didn't want to book 'im if I could 'elp it. However, Jenks, the air-raid warden, cured 'im. 'I'll cure 'im,' says Jenks, and 'e up and 'eaves half a brick through the window next time 'e sees a light showing arter black-out. And when Moggridge comes out, breathin' fire and fury, Jenks says 'That's jest a sample o' wot'll 'appen one o' these days, only it'll be a bomb as'll bring the hole 'ouse down about your ears.' And

if old Moggy doesn't apologise an' behave 'imself arter that...
'ighly irregular way o' doin', o' course, but I overlooked it, sir,
seein' as the end was good. Another thing, too. Doesn't believe
in wot 'e calls 'divers weights and divers measures.' 'All of 'em an
h'abomination to the Lord,' 'e says. Pays 'is bills on the nail in
pounds, shillin's and pence, only. No sixpences, ten-bob notes
or such. Just pound notes, shillin's and coppers. No bank
cheques for 'im, given or taken. *And* he won't reckernise
Summer Time and put 'is clocks on. No fear. Proper nuisance 'e
is with 'is religion. But straight as a die...an' when a man's
straight, it makes up for a lot... Good arternoon, sir... Nice to
see yer in these parts... Gooooood arternoon."

Nankivell pedalled off furiously lest the loquacious bobby
should open more floodgates of information. On the way he
smiled to think that if you know where to go for knowledge, it
saves you a lot of trouble. If he had only thought of the garru-
lous Lugg, he'd have solved his case long ago.

19

ROBINSON DOES HIS DUTY

The police had kept the fact that Doyle had been brought back to town as quiet as possible. He had travelled from Holyhead in a closed car and entered the police station by the side door. Nevertheless, the news got out and leaked all over Swarebridge. Mr Meister, during his visit to Nankivell, had heard Doyle's bawling protests from the cells and confidentially told his wife that he guessed who was there. The news reached Burt at five o'clock when he went to the club for a drink.

In cold blood, Burt would have shrunk from killing anyone. He feared the consequences too much, for he wished to go on living himself. He was, however, passionate and hot-blooded, bad-tempered, irritable and vindictive. He had risen from poverty in the lowest parts of Swarebridge to comfort and security as a principal tradesman and town councillor. He was always on the look-out for snubs, signs of patronage, and opposition to his progress from those who knew his origins. For the most part, all his grievances were imaginary; his so-called betters admired his enterprise when, as a young man, he launched out on his own and worked day and night to build up his business. But in his eagerness to get on and make his mark,

167

he married above him. Mrs Burt was a little lady, and he must have swept her off her feet in a weak moment. He should have married a woman of his own type, who would have returned blow for blow but worked her fingers to the bone in the shop. Mrs Burt bowed her head to every storm and kept as far away from the meat as she could.

It was not long before Burt was heard declaring that he liked a woman with a bit of spirit and shortly after, he was out searching for one; in fact, a succession of them. On one side, he was prepared to fight to the death, like his own bulldogs, against any threat to the position he had carved for himself; and on the other, he grew less and less physically equipped through gross living to do so calmly. Intent on bolstering-up his fortunes, he took advantage of the war-time situation to create an extensive underground market and when Harbuttle stumbled across it, Burt's passions got the better of him.

Once involved in murder, Burt began feverishly to cover his tracks. He had not intended to kill Willie Pole any more than he had originally intended to murder Harbuttle. He tried at first to find out what the youngster knew, and when Willie began to howl, he lost his temper and control and madly stifled the boy's cries.

With his alibi and his keeping in the background at Zion, Burt might have got away with it, had not the police stumbled by accident on what was happening at Toad-in-Hole.

When he heard that Doyle was in the cells, Burt lost his head. His nerve had gradually been going since he had visited the farm and found the Irishman gone. He hoped the flight would throw suspicion on the cattle dealer and that the police wouldn't find him. If they did, Doyle was sure to squeal. As a last resort, the unhappy murderer decided, he would hang himself. Meanwhile, he remained, like one fascinated, in Sware-bridge waiting for news of Doyle.

Burt's heart seemed to leap out of his chest when he heard

that the Irishman was in the local jail. He gripped the edge of the bar for support, for the blood surged into his brain in hot waves. He drank his whisky hastily and then hurried across the street to his garage, his impulse to run like mad barely controlled by a cunning thought that he might manage to make a successful break-away. With trembling fingers, Burt unlocked the double-doors and started the car. Then, he rushed into his shop by the back way, opened the safe and stuffed all the money he could find in his pockets. When he returned to his car, Nankivell and Patchett were standing beside it. Burt made straight for them...

"Burt, I'd like a word or two..." Nankivell got no further. The butcher's great fist caught Patchett on the point of the jaw and dropped him on the cobblestones. Nankivell instinctively raised his guard as Burt's fist shot out again. The Superintendent side-stepped, but too late. The blow missed his jaw but caught him under the left ear and sent him staggering into the depths of the garage. In a flash Burt was in the car and off, careering madly down the High Street, past the protesting constable on point duty, and out into the open road.

* * *

WEDNESDAY AFTERNOON IS HALF-CLOSING in Swarebridge and the shop men of the Home Guard fall-in for duties and manoeuvres. On this of all days, two Italian prisoners were at large, and all posts and roadblocks were manned. At the Sticksey Road blockhouse, Corporal Albert Robinson, a salesman in Pitfoddle's Drapery Stores, was holding the fort with two other colleagues. To the great disgust of travellers, this trio were stopping all traffic and examining papers. They had already been through four crowded buses from end to end and halted about two dozen private cars. Thanks to their diligence, a harmless escaping lunatic had been restored to the Swarebridge

Asylum, and now they were having a bit of bother with the mail van.

"You got no right to 'old-up His Majesty's Mails," protested the driver, who knew Corporal Robinson well, for they were members of the same bowling club. Postman Phelps was in no mood for being bossed by the perfectly civil Robinson, whom, to use his own words he "could make rings round at bowling, blindfolded at that."

"Now, Cyril," said Robinson, "You know we've got to do our duty. Everybody to be treated alike. Fair-do's, Cyril, fair-do's."

"It's not fair at all, Albert," replied Phelps aggressively. "I got this run to do accordin' to schedule and 'ere you are 'olding me up."

"Well, just let me see your Identity Card, that's all. You know, unbeknown to you, these escaped prisoners might be in among your bags. Let's have a look and then you can be off."

"That's my identity card, see?" said Phelps, pointing to the golden Royal monogram on his van.

The argument ended there for the time being, however, for the attention of the three Home Guards was taken by a car furiously approaching from Swarebridge. One of the privates ran into the middle of the road, his hand stiffly raised in a halting gesture. The car did not slacken and only by leaping for his life did the guardsman avoid being flattened on the tarmac.

"Halt!!!" yelled Robinson, rushing back to the blockhouse and emerging with his rifle. The car was well away. Carefully Corporal Robinson sighted and fired. He had been Home Guarding since the LDV days and knew his business. The car seemed to take leave of its senses and pursued a crazy career on the road surface for a brief minute, then, just where, in days long gone, Pogsley's car had halted so momentously on the bridge over the Sware, it plunged madly, struck the parapet of the bridge and somersaulted into space, coming to rest with a crash in the river bed.

As Robinson ran breathlessly to the scene, Dr Percival's car, which Nankivell had commandeered in the High Street, drew level with the blockhouse and the shaken superintendent and a constable emerged.

* * *

THERE WAS little water in the Sware but that did more harm than good to Burt. He was dying when they reached him. Blood dribbled from his open mouth and he moaned as they tried to move him.

"Leave me... Don't move me... I'm all in," he whispered. "Sorry, Nankivell, sorry... It was me did it, both of them... I don't know, I don't know...what came over me..." And with that, he vomited blood and collapsed. He died that night in Swarebridge Infirmary, where, not far away, Patchett was just beginning to take an interest in his whereabouts again.

20

PEACE AGAIN

We are back in Zion again. A month has passed since the bloodthirsty events of the Swarebridge murders cast their shadows over that happy Ebenezer, but any stranger finding himself in today's gathering would be surprised if he were told that but a few short weeks ago, commotion and bloodshed prevailed where now is peace and order. Thus time does its healing work.

They are holding their annual November Bazaar, and all the world of Zion is there, crowding in the large schoolroom, chattering, prattling, trucking and trading. The men wear buttonholes of Michaelmas daisies and other seasonable blooms and have paid dearly for them to the coy young girls who busily hawk them about, and frequently return for more to the flower stall, over which those two blossoms, Muriel Arrowsmith and Mary O'Dare, now fully reconciled, are presiding with great enthusiasm.

Soft glances are exchanged between several of the remaining young men and the many girls who, with sparkling eyes and flushed cheeks, sell this and that at outrageous prices. This sentimental warmth is gently fanned by a string band, a quintet to be precise, presided over by Mr Meister who had offered his services on the cello, and he is supported by a languid pianist and by his two daughters, the younger of which has taken the place of Tilly Burt on second violin and now blushes every time she catches the ardent gaze of Stanley Butterfield as the bow of his viola comes and goes. After all, the annual bazaar is also Zion's busiest marriage mart and many of those who have worked amicably together for so long in aid of the chapel funds, will soon announce their decisions to make a life job of the partnerships. Mr Meister is filled with *Sehnsucht* as he watches the electric glances come and go across the instruments. Now and then, he thinks of Tilly Burt and of Schubert's Quintet in C, abandoned, alas, perhaps for good.

"How *is* poor Mrs Burt?" asks Mrs Maw, the deacon's wife, of Mrs Wildbore, whose husband is a magistrate.

"Still with her sister, in London, poor dear. She's getting over it a bit I hear but will never return here. You've heard about Tilly?"

"*No*...what of her?" And the two good ladies go into a huddle. Others on the fringe turn their ears eagerly in their direction whilst pretending to be interested elsewhere.

"She and young Johnny Friar are shortly to be married. Now *I do* like the way Johnny's stuck to her through it all...*a nice boy*... Mrs Burt and Tilly will be living together until Johnny is demobilised from the RAF after the war... By the way, have you heard the latest about the Leatherbarrows...?"

The conversation subsides into undertones, greatly to the annoyance of the pirate listeners, who now draw apart to criticise Mrs Maw's hat.

Mr Joshua Butterfield, the new director of Pogsley's, is, as the man with Zion's money bags, a most interested party in the present proceedings. With a wintry smile, the best he ever can muster, he keeps popping in and out of the small classroom in which his staff collect the proceeds of sales and count and enter them. Mr Butterfield's nose is redder and more pinched than ever in his enthusiasm and each time the mounting totals are announced to him, he rubs his hands and bares his teeth, for he has guaranteed an overdraft for Zion at the bank and today's effort is surely going to liquidate it and free him from his bond.

Mrs Butterfield, seated in a large, reinforced chair, is like a queen presiding over a retinue of very pretty handmaidens. In her capacity as president of the refreshment stall, she is chief sales official. This stall is an evergreen source of trouble, and the ferment caused by Mrs Joshua's behaviour at one bazaar is only just being lived down at the next, and so on in perpetuity. Here it is, going on again under our noses. At small tables set round the refreshment stall, sit the notables of the town, such as Mrs Pogsley-Smythe, who has just put her foot in it by declaring this *Rummage* open, and Mrs Fingerbowle, wife of the sitting MP for Swarebridge and Sticksey. These tables are reserved for the élite and the lowlier ones of Zion are crowded out to a classroom, there to dine at the long boards which we have before encountered. In a democratic body such as Zion, it's all wrong to make fish of one and stone of another. This year, thanks to Mrs Pogsley-Smythe's gaffe, the smouldering resentment looks like bursting into flames when the ladies meet together for the inquest after the bazaar. Furthermore, where have the two dozen eggs, presented to the stall by Mr Moggridge, gone to...? Haven't even been displayed! It's to be hoped that Mrs Pogsley-Smythe...

Mrs Nankivell and Mrs Percival are running the ladies' stall, which deals in articles of infant and female attire and allure. In these days of coupons, this is a hard task, but accomplished by scheming and scraping and the tireless efforts of Miss Sleaford, who stands modestly at the back of the stall, hidden from view by a curtain composed of bath towels, pillowslips and forms of ladies' wear which may be displayed without immodesty. Miss Sleaford has just snatched from its moorings a freely flaunted piece of intimate lingerie which has hitherto escaped her censorship and she conceals it beneath the stall. A procession of women comes and goes in Miss Sleaford's retreat, like initiates visiting the oracle, and in secret she displays and sells what must in public be withheld from the masculine eye.

In one corner of the room Mr Wildbore, JP, has condescended temporarily to superintend the pitch-ring game. There for two pence a try you get three rings, which if slung successively on hooks totalling twenty will bring you as reward a packet of five Woodbines. That little nonentity Mr Meers has suddenly discovered a new skill and is filling his pockets with cigarettes! Mr Wildbore, who suspects Meers of practising for the occasion in the rear of his little shop, contemplates turning over supervision to the menace but he fears a rebuff...

When the evening has far advanced and Mr Butterfield's cash bags are filled to overflowing, a diversion occurs. Someone enters the room and is immediately surrounded by a battling throng of women. Terrified, the men begin to wonder if another outbreak of hostilities is imminent. But no. It is only the Rev Partington, who has been absent from town on urgent domestic business and returns to the fold full of smiles.

The women are clamouring the same question in a hundred different ways. Muriel Arrowsmith, who has been preserving a posy for the occasion, approaches and is fended-off by a protective and determined cohort of matrons.

"A little girl..." says Partington, and a scene follows which reminds us of a football match at which the favourite centre-forward has netted the ball. There is a mad rush to the ladies' stall, where articles of infant attire are passed or torn from hand to hand. Mr Maw, the deacon with the most initiative, has already begun to pass round the hat for the benefit of young Miss Partington. Then and there, the Rev B Augustus decides to stay at Zion for the rest of his life. His shrivelled faith, watered by this fountain of charity, bursts into vigorous blooming again and the desert of his soul blossoms as the rose.

Nothing but unsaleable odds and ends, dirty paper, empty bags, ice-cream cartons and cigarette packets, and a few trampled buttonhole-blooms remain of the day's splendour when Nankivell and Dr Percival meet again to take home their wives. Butterfield has gone off in triumph to deposit in the night safe of the bank a phenomenal bagful and Mrs Butterfield has departed leaving someone else to deal with a terrifying pile of dirty dishes from her stall. The hatted helpers have carted these off to the sinks with many lamentations and threats against Mrs Joshua. One of them utters a little scream and points to a number of carving knives assembled after a good day's work.

"What does that remind you of, Mrs Clewer?" she whispers in awful tones.

"Don't be so soft..." replies Mrs C, and plunges her arms up to the elbows in soapy water and dirty pots.

In the main hall Miss Sleaford is bidding the Superintendent goodnight. She shakes him by the hand cordially.

"...a splendid result," she says, and then wistfully, "How pleased Alderman Harbuttle would have been... He always finished off the bazaar with follow-my-leader..."

A gust of wind blows open the door, scattering the stray pieces of paper, catching up the petals and leaves of the broken rosettes, and wildly agitating the ornamental palms and aspidistras of the barren stalls. Miss Sleaford stands horrified at the words which have so wantonly escaped her. The air feels cold and damp, and outside, the setter, which Nankivell has tied to a doorknob to await him, howls miserably for human company.

HE'D RATHER BE DEAD

AN INSPECTOR LITTLEJOHN MYSTERY

GEORGE BELLAIRS

1

THE MAN WHO ROSE FROM NOTHING

Perhaps someday a worthy biographer will write the life story of Sir Gideon Ware as a signpost to guide the young to success.

Here, however, we are mainly concerned with his death, which occurred at the height of his fame and fortune and shook the country from end to end.

Gideon Ware was born in Hull. We know nothing of his parents, for he never mentioned them in after life, except to tell how they threw him out at the age of twelve to earn his own living. At twenty, he was a bricklayer. At twenty-three, he left Hull for personal reasons and turned up at Westcombe. He was sixty when he was murdered at the banquet he was giving to celebrate his election as mayor of the place.

In its early days, Westcombe was a highly respectable, almost austere resort. Frequented by select little family parties, who boarded at very sedate establishments on the sea front and came year after year at exactly the same period. A small, rough promenade, a few bathing huts and very discreet Pierrots. Little else. By ten o'clock in the evening, the children were all in bed, their elders indoors preparing to retire, and the whole town peaceful and quiet.

Look at it now, as left by its benefactor, Sir Gideon Ware!

It has absorbed its neighbours one after another with insatiable appetite.

Miles of level, concrete promenade fronting an area five times that of the original borough. Acres of pleasure beach, embracing every kind of device for human entertainment and sensation. Huge hotels, cinemas, theatres, ballrooms, bars. Enormous restaurants and railway stations. During the season, the latter can hardly hold the vast throngs which come and go from and to every part of England.

Shouting, singing, brawling, and dancing go on until the small hours of the morning.

Nothing remains of the original Westcombe but the quaint little harbour, which the mushroom town has thrust aside like a poor relation, down by the riverbank, where the fishermen take home their boats at night after days of pleasure tripping.

When first he arrived in Westcombe, where bricklayers were temporarily in demand, Ware called at a small beer-house and there, over a pot of ale, overheard two men arranging to buy land for development. Gideon left his beer and somehow contrived to secure an option before the pair of jerry-builders. He made two hundred pounds out of the deal; and that was the beginning. After that, Gideon Ware set about Westcombe with a will!

He might not, of course, have remained so firmly wedded to the place but for an accident. In 1913, Ware tried his luck elsewhere, overstepped the mark, and became bankrupt. By that time, he was a member of clubs in various parts of the country. When disgrace came his way, those august institutions, metaphorically speaking, passed by on the other side. Each of them accepted his resignation from membership before he had time to tender it.

All except the Westcombe Constitutional Club. Its committee were so busy cashing in on the building boom that they quite forgot to blackball Gideon. *He* never forgot it. He thought of the WCC as his friend indeed, and when he re-made his fortunes and earned a knighthood in 1918 by building huts for the Government, he made straight for his old haunts, settled down there for good, and gave the WCC the finest headquarters that money could buy.

He then set out to put Westcombe on the map, and, by Jove, he did it with a vengeance! Look at the posters on every hoarding and the hundreds of thousands of guidebooks annually scattered nationwide!

Sir Gideon would not, however, join the town council until he had had enough of building and finance and decided to retire and become a gentleman. Then he put up and was elected. Two years later, he became Mayor, long before his rightful turn.

And now, we take steps to be in at the death.

It is about noon on a sunny day in August. The awning is out over the door and approach of the Town Hall at Westcombe. The red official carpet has been unrolled on the steps and the corporation silver plate has been taken from the bank and laid on the tables of the banqueting hall. This is the day on which His Worship the Mayor gives his annual lunch to the Borough officials.

A number of holiday making sightseers have gathered in knots on the pavement, and two policemen have arranged them in orderly and becoming lines. When, however, the audience discovers that the Prime Minister or, at least, the Regional Commissioner is not expected, but only the Mayor and retinue, they begin to melt away. They can see such palavering at home any day!

By old custom in Westcombe, the officials honour the Mayor by a dinner each November after his election. His Worship returns the compliment in August, when visitors are in full spate and are in the mood to gasp and gape and say how wonderful it all is.

This Year of Grace 1942, it is to be something special. For, whenever Sir Gideon Ware does anything, he beats the band. This time *No Expense Spared* and Black Markets shriek from the menu.

Hors d'oeuvres.
Barley Cream Soup or Clear Cold.
Fillets of Sole Mornay. Anchovy Sauce.
Lamb Cutlets and Peas. Fried Potatoes.
Cold Chicken and Tongue.
Cold Asparagus. Salads. Tomatoes.
Fruit Tart and Cream.
Charlotte Russe.
Bombe Gideon.
Cheese. Celery. Fruits. Coffee.

Canon Silvester Wallopp, incumbent of the largest church in Westcombe, could not resist it! An epicure of the first water, he had firmly decided to give the lunch a miss, but when he saw the menu (the chef, who was a member of his flock, let him have a peep) he gave in.

The Canon has been deeply offended by the Mayor. Hitherto, he has been Mayor's Chaplain, *ex officio*. Ware is a Roman Catholic, but instead of appointing the priest, Father Manfred, has picked the Rev Titus Gaukroger, head of the Beach Mission, if you please! "He's put religion on the map in Westcombe," said Sir Gideon. "Honour where honour's due, I always say." And it was so.

Canon Wallopp is by far the most imposing of the guests. Six feet and clad in fine raiment. A heavy, round red face with roving little eyes. Viewed through the golden glass of the vestibule where we first meet him, wondering where he's left his ticket of invitation and fuming inwardly because he can't enter without it, he looks like a dogfish in aspic. Some toady once told him he was the image of Cardinal Wolsey. Later, our friend Inspector Littlejohn is to notice in him a strong resemblance to a casual alcoholic tout who shouts loudly in front of a cheap-jack-auctioneer's shop on the promenade. The Canon is a bachelor, too, and very partial to innocuous dalliance with young ladies, like the warden of a seraglio, or as he himself expresses it, *in loco parentis*.

Now, the Canon walks eagerly into the dining hall, cutting dead on the way the Official Chaplain and Father Manfred, slips on the polished floor and measures his length. Fortunately, this accident in no way impairs his appetite, for he later gormandises his way steadily through all the courses, alternatives and all.

The great hall of the Municipal Buildings is fine and spacious, the embodiment of the prosperity of a community which derives its extensive revenues from its enterprises. The dining tables are dwarfed by their surroundings, Lilliputian, and are in the centre of the polished parquet on which Canon Wallopp has just come a cropper. Tall pillars of waxed sycamore, exquisitely grained, soar upwards to an arched roof, further enlarged by a great dome of transparent golden glass, which adds the tint of sunny wine to whatever kind of light penetrates through it.

On a dais at one end of the room, Sid Simmons and his Ten Hot Dogs play swing music. Sid is the permanent attraction at the Westcombe Winter Gardens (open from April until October only!) and has brought his "boys" and their hideous noises to honour the Mayor, free of charge. As the party enters, the maestro raises his silver trumpet to the heavens in ecstasy and, wringing his body in a series of awful convulsions, stamping his feet, and rolling his eyes, flings his own arrangement of Liszt's *Liebestraum* in a hundred cacophonous bits all over the place. Mr

Cuthbert Acron, Mus Bac, the town organist, takes Sid aside and reminds him that this is a solemn civic function, not a Saturnalia. Thereafter, the maestro is in difficulties, for like certain cooks, he cannot concoct a straight dish, but specialises in garnishing existing stuff in odious or exotic trappings. He lays aside his trumpet sadly and for the rest of the time grimaces and waves his hands at the boys who distastefully and unsteadily plough through Strauss waltzes and polkas by Offenbach.

A congratulatory group gathers round the Mayor. They shake his hand and exchange pleasant or barbed greetings. Sir Gideon makes for the high table and takes his place. Like a flock of rooks alighting, the rest seem somehow to shake themselves into order in next to no time.

Sir Gideon is clad in his official garb. Purple robes trimmed with scarlet and ermine. Cocked hat and chain of office, the latter with a gold link, an inch long, for every Mayor since the creation of the borough — thirty-six of them. What it will be like at the centenary celebrations is a faint municipal nightmare already!

Ware is a stoutly built man of middle stature, with short arms and legs. Round, florid face, sandy moustache, dark mottled complexion and eyebrows like tufts of grey cotton wool. His nose is small, snub and thick at the roots. Low forehead, merging into a bald head with close-clipped white hair at the back. His eyes are grey, malicious and set in pouches of wrinkles. With a podgy hand he gestures to the head waiter to begin.

Mr Gaukroger looks outraged and disappointed. They are starting without saying grace!

Grace has been waived. So have many other things, including formal arrangement of seating in order of precedence. Sir Gideon has fixed that according to his own dictatorial tastes and sense of humour.

"No toasts either," he also said.

"Oh, just one, sir...or two. First 'The King.' One to you; and another to the guest of honour," deferentially suggested the Borough Treasurer and mayor's major-domo.

"All right, then. But no more. There's too many coming who like the sound of their own voices. If we get *them* going, we'll be here all night and I've work to do in the afternoon, if you other chaps haven't."

He was always hinting that the corporation officials were underworked and overpaid.

The high-table guests, who have been hanging round His Worship's chair and place, dissipate themselves to their proper seats as indicated in the plan by the door.

There, in his glory, sits Sir Gideon.

Then, to his right, the guest of honour, Mr Wilmott Saxby, chairman of the neighbouring Urban District Council of Hinster's Ferry. A square-set, little fellow, with a mop of white hair and a little white moustache. He looks surprised to find himself where he is.

Beyond Saxby, the Rev Titus Gaukroger, gaunt, bony, long faced and pale. With long, knobby fingers he clutches the water carafe specially placed before him, for he is fanatically TT. By his side at the extreme end of the table, Canon Wallopp cutting him dead and concentrating on the victuals.

At Sir Gideon's left hand is the Town Clerk, Mr Edgar Kingsley-Smith, a tall, lean, clever-looking solicitor and a member of an old Westcombe family. Next comes the Deputy-Mayor, plain Tom Hogg, one of three Socialists on the Council. A sturdy, forthright man is Tom, beloved of all the working classes, son of a fisherman and himself a carter until his trade union made him their secretary.

Lastly, Father Manfred. A long, cadaverous ascetic countenance, with burning eyes and no hair whatever on his head or face. This defect gives him a clean-swept, reptilian appearance.

A good friend and a terrible enemy, this Jesuit might be found any day chasing the alcoholic members of his flock from the pubs with a stick or walking along the promenade with six little boys and girls laughing on either hand. The sight of him in a street where Catholics are rioting brings an awful hush over the place, whilst children will rush from the houses yelling with joy and prattling to clutch the skirts of his cassock.

On the two arms which radiate from the high table are posted the lesser lights according to Sir Gideon's malicious sense of humour. Opposite Mr Oxendale, the bank manager, sits Mr Oliver, the Borough Treasurer, with whom he is always quarrelling about rates of interest and commission. Mrs Pettigrew, JP, Chairman of Magistrates and a member of the old aristocracy, faces Mr Pott-Wridley, Head of the Department of Dry Goods and Edible Oils, evacuated to Westcombe from London, and who has requisitioned Pettigrew Hall and forced Mrs Pettigrew to live over the stables. They cannot bear the sight of each other and glare ferociously through their transparent cold soup. The same applies to two other partners, Mr Harold Brown, the Magistrates' Clerk, who has been turned out of his spacious business premises by the Department of Poultry and Incubation, whose Principal is his *vis-a-vis*, Mr Ryder, OBE. Mr Boumphrey, the Chief Constable of Westcombe, alone is blessed by having no comrade in hate opposite him or by his side.

On the other arm of the tables, the Medical Officer of Health, McAndrew, frowns across at Liptrott, editor of the *Westcombe Gazette*, which has resisted his campaign against inadequate hospital accommodation in the Borough. Opposite Mr Openshaw, Borough Accountant, sits his implacable opponent on matters of expenditure, Mr Barcledyne, Chairman of the Westcombe Development Board. There follow Messrs Whyte, MA, and Budd, Headmaster of the Westcombe Grammar School and Chairman of the Pleasure Beach Proprietors' Alliance respectively, a pair like cat and dog — one very superior, the other grossly ignorant scholastically, and proud of it.

Beyond these, a medley of magisterial, municipal and administrative nonentities.

The only women present are officials of the town, and magistrates. Male diners are not accompanied by wives or other feminine counterparts. The women of Westcombe have taken this badly and are planning to boycott Lady Ware's "At Home" next Saturday, which means that they'll probably all turn up smiling.

A limited choice of wines has been brought to light from mysterious sources and circulates. The epicure is not impressed, for whilst the quality of some is good, they are served indiscriminately, without regard to the dish accompanying them.

Those at the high table drink from ceremonial silver goblets, the freak gift of a past mayor anxious to impress. That of Sir Gideon bears the Corporation's arms in fine enamel. It is the mayor's cup! The lesser lights lower down drink from glass vessels.

Oswald, the head waiter, has given the signal. His underlings begin to deploy and circulate like planets round the sun. They must be subject, like the orbs of heaven, to some law, but only Oswald seems to know it. They race hither and thither, sweating, running, serving with little jerky movements which convulse the whole of their bodies. At any time, one expects them to rise from the floor and fly over and around the guests like winged Mercuries, dropping the courses like manna on their plates.

Soup. Joint. Sweets. The tail-end of the repast. They all come and go. Canon Wallopp ploughs through them. Now he's busy at the asparagus, like a conjurer who has swallowed a hard-boiled egg and immediately afterwards tugs from his gullet the flags of all nations. Again, pecking at the celery, like a huge, corpulent parrot at a chunk of cuttlefish. Noisily, too. Clickety-

GEORGE BELLAIRS

chup. Clickety-chup. Gulp. Like those of a voracious earwig the great mandibles of the Canon chew their way through Sir Gideon's eatables.

The board is cleared. Coffee, and cigars for those who speak in time. Cigarettes for the rest.

The toast "The King" is drunk with enthusiasm.

Mr Kingsley-Smith is on his feet. The town clerk is a good speaker. Calm and polished. But he is not too comfortable at present. Sir Gideon is a difficult one to whom to hand bouquets or render thanks. Still, as head official, Mr Kingsley-Smith must rise to the occasion. He balances himself on his heels, slips a nonchalant hand in his pocket and beams around.

"Mr Mayor, ladies and gentlemen..."

And he goes on to look here, upon this picture, and on this. Westcombe before Ware; Westcombe after...and so on. Like an advertisement for a patent medicine.

All the time, Sir Gideon regards him with a twisted smile, mingling pride of achievement with scorn for the orator.

"...and raise your glasses with me in a toast to our Mayor, Sir Gideon Ware. His Worship the Mayor!"

There is a shuffling of feet and a scraping of chairs. The Canon just manages to raise himself by swinging on the table.

"HIS WORSHIP THE MAYOR!"

The crowd mutters it like a response in church.

The clatter subsides.

Sir Gideon rises. He doesn't look well. His face is pale, and he seems like one in the first stages of influenza. Whether he has taken a chill, too much wine, or the food's a bit "off", it is hard to say. However, he rallies.

Ware's diction is good. Not in vain has he spent a few hundred pounds and five years' study on courses in elocution and "the art of psychological speech." His private secretary, too, is a past-master of speech writing.

He renders formal thanks and then turns to his right-hand neighbour and proposes "Our Visitors."

Mr Wilmott Saxby gives Sir Gideon a sidelong, upward glance. He has not been brought here for nothing and well he knows it! Hinster's Ferry is the last UDC in the district to hold out against the encroachments of the new Westcombe. In the river Swaine, Hinster's Ferry has its "moat," its protection against the assaults of the sprawling, upstart resort. It is a small fishing village, with little or no promenade, but a certain type of visitors like it immensely, for it is quiet and unspoiled. A tiny harbour with a few yachts, an annual regatta, good fishing in the river and the Swaine Deep beyond, and little besides. The ferry-boat crosses every quarter-hour, taking visitors to and fro, and the last one goes at ten-thirty. After that a deep peace descends, broken only by the sea and the rustle of winds across the salt flats. Hitherto the river has acted as a sanitary cordon against the vulgarity of Westcombe.

Sir Gideon, unable to extend the promenade and absorb the tempting resort over the water, wants to build a bridge, and the Hinster's Ferry UDC, headed by Mr Wilmott Saxby, have resisted like mad, and with success.

But when Sir Gideon is intent on anything, he concentrates every power of his mind, wind, limb, and purse on the task.

Wilmott Saxby is the bastion. For years he's held out. To yield would ruin Hinster's Ferry and all its charm. But lately, Ware has been gradually getting his yes-men on the UDC. In fact, Wilmott Saxby has now only a majority of one on his side against the amalgamation and the bridge.

Is Ware now going to announce publicly his final triumph?

"...of course, Mr Wilmott Saxby and I differ on minor matters. Who doesn't? For example, the joining of our two communities and the building of a bridge..." (loud laughter).

Sir Gideon pauses. What's the matter? He eases his collar,

mops his sweating brow, and wipes his lips. He clutches the table and, by a supreme effort of will, goes on.

"You all know I'm a man of progress. Progress. Progress. Progress or perish. As Pericles said, 'We do not copy our neighbours; we are an example to them.' Rather than stagnate...rather than stagnate..."

He is in great distress. The Town Clerk rises and fills a goblet with Mr Gaukroger's water. Ware waves it aside.

"Stagnate! I'd rather be dead!"

And with that, he collapses, slips down in his chair, sprawls there for a moment and slides to the floor beneath the table.

The assembly rises in great confusion. McAndrew, the Medical Officer, rushes to Sir Gideon's side and they move the Mayor behind his chair. Ware is convulsed. His body arches and becomes shockingly contorted. His breath comes and goes with great labour and in painful jerks.

"Is it a fit?" asks Wilmott Saxby.

Hastily, the doctor sends the first man he sees as he raises his head for the ambulance.

"We must get him to hospital right away..."

"What's the matter, McAndrew?" asks the Town Clerk with a trace of impatience.

But the MO is not committing himself. It is Father Manfred who breaks the tense silence.

"Looks like strychnine to me, doctor."

McAndrew purses his lips and nods. He has sent for his bag to his room in the building and this arrives just as the orderlies from the ambulance enter with their stretcher. Even as they bear out the wretched Ware, the doctor continues in his efforts to administer an emetic.

The Chief Constable, a heavy, officious man, takes charge of the situation.

"Close all the doors," he bawls. "Nobody's to leave unless I say so."

"Where are *you* going, Father Manfred? Nobody's to leave."

But the priest thrusts him aside.

"I am going where I'll be needed before Sir Gideon reaches his journey's end," he says and strides from the place with purposeful steps and enters the ambulance with the patient.

The good priest was right. On the way, Sir Gideon Ware died.

Made in the USA
Middletown, DE
04 April 2020